Beware
of
snakes!

Thanks

[signature]

"The only happiness I ever knew was as a boy surfing Malibu."

- J. Paul Getty

Also by Fred Reiss
Insult And Live!
How To Insult And Abuse Everyone

Copyright 1995

ISBN Number: 0-9623869-1-X

The lyrics to "Surfer Joe" used by generous permission from copyright claimants Miraleste Music Co. 50 percent and Robin Hood music 50 percent. Copyright year 1963. Writer. Ron Wilson.

The lyrics to "Do It Again" Copyright 1966. Renewed 1994, Irving Music, Inc. (BMI). All rights reserved International copyright secured. Use by permission.

The lyrics to "I Just Wasn't Made For These Times" Copyright 1968 Irving Music, Inc. (BMI) All rights reserved International copyright secured. Used by permission.

No kook, surfer, or any character in this highly fictional and satirical book resembles or is based on anyone living or dead.

Cover:
Frank Doyle of Silicon Graphics and a true childhood friend.

Author and cover and contents photo by Wayne Kenney.

Published in the United States of America by:
Santa Cruz'n Press
PO Box 3523
Santa Cruz, Ca. 95062

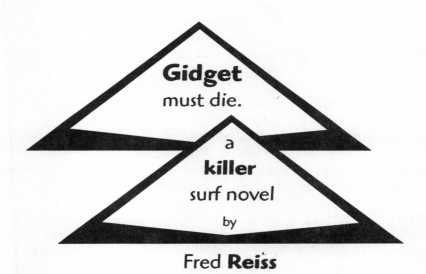

Gidget
must die.

a
killer
surf novel
by

Fred **Reiss**

Special thanks page:

To my dad, mom, brother, and two sisters.

To my girlfriend Laurie Roberts for her devotional support.

To Pat Farley and Wayne Kenney, because without their friendship I would have never been able to write this book.

Al Baggett for his detonation knowledge (Any errors are mine not his.).

To Frank Doyle, for his time, creativity, and help. (And Leslie)

Ken Dixon for editorial help and covering for my meals.

And to the friendship and generosity of Mike Eaton and Hap Jacobs for the margaritas and the boards they shaped for me.

To the Floyds: Dan, Craig and Debbie, for their support and time.

And to the Santa Cruz'n soul surfers who have shared waves, beach burgers, and their lives, as well as tolerated my surfing: Hal Stanger, Randi Fish, Terry Arnaud, Larry Freitas, Thomas Farley, Terry Simms, Antonio Drexel, Jeff Maldanado, Cort Gion, Kevin Randick, Palma Formica, Marcel Soros, Duncan Kennedy, Mike Medina, Michelle and Jeff Scott, Katie Loudon, Jim Colford, Bobby Behrns, Brad Bishop, Pete Olamit, Brenda Leys, Curt Skelton, Heather and Dane Gray, Andre Hart, Ron Edwards, Jim Ferdinand, Tim Burke, Jennifer, Carrie, and Jeanette Schraeder, George Dumas, Phil Dirt, Gary Kammerer, Dan Michaels, Bobby Ackerley, Allan Bargo, Mark Olsen, Francis Farley, Ed Cavallo, Johnny and Rosemary Rice, Bobby Mills, Cliff Ellyn, Linda Dominco, John Sibailia, Jim Stone, Pat Simms, Beverly Lindquist, Jim Montgomery, Charlie Bursey, Bob Dobbs, Judy Eastman, Marshal Krase, Greg Adams, Glen Viguers. Suzanna Wittpenn, Bud Clark, Dave Hein, Peter Meyer, Doug McNae, Chris Thorpe, Stretch Riedle, Debbie Szasz, Allan Reilly, Kit Santaella, Valerie Hopkins, Stu Wright, surf shop rats Garrett and Josh, and all the different customers who have wandered into the Santa Cruz'n Surf Shop and told me their views on life and surfing.

Contents

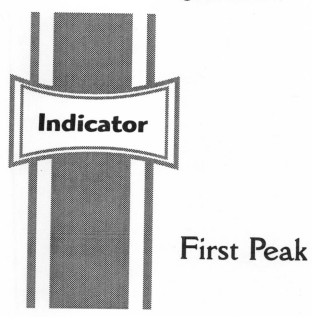

Indicator

First Peak

I'm writing this book because I've always had a nostalgic tidal pull toward a time period I never lived. A period where the Malibu Pit Crew surfed uncrowded perfection in clean blue California waters during the forties and the fifties. They paddled away from America's most prosperous economic times. The Pit Crew didn't care. They just surfed. Malibu was wide open then. They drank cheap wine and waffled girls in the shade of a palm-frond shack. They slept on the beach at night, lived out of beaten-up trucks and cars with boarded-up windows. They earned money renting surfboards, collecting deposit bottles, or finding change in the sand. They ate abalone, lobster, crabs, and rock cod. Still, even though I'm closer to forty than thirty years old, I'll take them over the present. I don't care whether the Malibu Pit Crew's world was real or misconceived, an escapist subculture, or whatever shorthand phrase the limited and frustrated use to dismiss the pulse of a fulfilled dream. Yes, and even knowing what I know now, I'll still take their Malibu world over anything.

Water is the fire of desire.

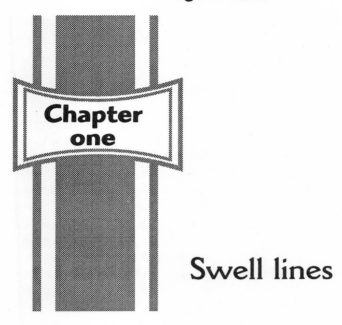

Chapter one

Swell lines

From the Journal of Surfer Joe

The Bu. Malibu, Maleewa, Humaliwu. It was ruined four times.

The first time it was ruined by the Spanish merchants and missionaries who discovered the home of the Chumash Indians in 1542. The Chumash were a peaceful tribe that lived along the shores of The Malibu. Their houses were spherical thatched huts. They fished from pine-plank and red yucca canoes, which were decorated with shells. The mountains along the coast protected and isolated the Chumash from The Valley inhabitants. The sage, sumac, and chaparral covered land abounded with grizzlies, elk, and mountain lions.

The generous tribe welcomed the Spanish explorers. The conquistadors took the natives' skills, arts, and land. In exchange, the Chumash were given Christianity, penal servitude, syphilis, and pneumonia. The Chumash didn't adapt to the customs of this New Spain. Many Chumash women gave themselves abortions instead of birthing children into an altered world of tampered tomorrows. The missionaries' "work" to reform these maritime pagans completely destroyed the Indians (The last full-blooded Chumash died in the nineteen fifties.).

Valley Kooks: 1.

Malibu: 0.

The twenty-two miles of coastline between Santa Monica and Ventura became a land grant given from Spanish King Charles III to Don Jose Bartolema in 1800, who renamed it Topanga Malibu Sequit, after the names of three Indian villages that once occupied the site. Bartolema's son, Tiburncio Tapai calculatingly appraised the secluded stretch of curved beach, and the large fresh water creek flowing down from the Santa Monica mountains. The range had two-thousand foot summits, which were pocketed with remote coves, canyons, and caves. Tapai used this isolated port of entry to smuggle and conceal gold, silver, liquor, and jewels. Unbribed officials wanted their cut of the Malibu smuggler's tax-free plunder. They tried to arrest Tapai. He eluded them but died during the chase. Tapai never revealed his hiding spot.

After the land became a United States territory in 1848, Malibu went through a few owners, among them, Matthew Keller, who renamed Malibu beach Keller's Cove. He used the flatlands for crops and brought in livestock. But the last owner of Malibu's 13,000 acres was Frederick Hastings Rindge, the son of a Massachusetts woolen merchant who inherited a fortune. He purchased The Bu in the late 1800's. Rindge built a ranch, used the land for grazing and farming, and put up a four-hundred foot pier for shipping. Rindge even had his own private railroads, the Hueneme and Malibu, which prevented any public access from the Southern Pacific Railroad. The Valley Kooks still came. They traveled through the Bu to points North or South on a road that was only passable during low tide. These kooks left garbage, stole the Rindge's pigs and cattle, and eventually destroyed the entire ranch with a blaze caused by one of their campfires. Shortly after the fire, an equally spent Rindge, died in 1905.

Valley Kooks: 2

Malibu: 0

After Rindge's death, his wife Rhonda May Rindge decided to bar kooks from passing through her restored Malibu. She had armed patrols drive off trespassers. This is what led to the third fall of The Bu. In 1908, the State of California wanted to run a highway through the upper hills above the Rindge beach estate. But, she didn't. May Rindge blew up roads, planted alfalfa in the ruts, built fences, and even had her guards shoot a few government surveyors. And when the killing didn't work, Rindge undertook an even more ruthless and immoral tactic, she hired lawyers. This dragged on for years. Her son eventually took *her* to court. He claimed May was incompetent to run the family's affairs because she spent one million dollars a year on lawsuits. He lost. In 1926, she lost. The courts ruled the Roosevelt Highway was to be built. She wanted $9,180,000 from the government for use of her land, they gave her $107,288. Out of bureaucratic spite, officials decided to run the road not above but *through* the Rindge coastline estate. Yet, May still continued to fight California in the courts. In an effort to pay her legal bills from four state supreme court and two US Supreme Court rulings, Rindge leased her land for a development called The Malibu Colony, but her mismanaged real estate company went bankrupt in 1929, and forced her to sell parcels of her Malibu estate. More and more Hollywood stars moved to The Colony area; in fact, in 1933, a bad actor, walked naked into Malibu and drowned ("A Star is Born."). May Rindge became a recluse and died in a room of her mansion in 1941. She was 75 and never saw her estate completely developed. Shortly after Rindge's death, her investment firm, the Marblehead Land Co., sold the twenty-four miles of property on both sides of the highway along the coast. Over the next several years the State of California was able to purchase Rindge's land for public beaches and parks. Her company still holds the valuable inland grazing rights. In 1942, the Rindge pier was destroyed by a storm. A private firm built a seven-hundred foot pier, and, at the end of the pier, constructed a twin two-story Cape Cod building (The firm sold the pier to the state in 1980.). You just can't deny the public excess.

Valley Kooks: 3.

Malibu: 0.

The final time Malibu was ruined, it was my Malibu. I'm talking about a privileged surf spot thirty-five miles Northwest of LA (pronounced Hell-Lay). My Malibu was an animated half-mile crescent of beach from the pier to the farthest outside third point reef. Perfect waves peeled to a surfer's right for nearly one thousand feet. It was in this haven the Malibu Pit Crew and I had perfection all to ourselves in the forties and the fifties. This Pit Crew was responsible for developing the surfboard as well as a classic style of surfing that stressed riding the pocket, graceful fades, noseriding, and drop-knee turns. But, then *she* came: Sally Koolner, alias The Gidget. She was a teenage girl who infiltrated The Pit Crew. Her stepfather, Francis Koolner, was a public relations hack for his father's real estate company. She informed Koolner about us, and because he knew some Hollywood people, saw a chance to write a book about the beach scene that might become a movie. It worked. A film, "The Gidget," was released in 1959. With the popularity of The Gidget, and surf music, every Valley Kook wanted to look cool, talk like a surfer, ride waves, and have luaus at the beach. The state bulldozed Toobsteak's gin-bottle strewn beach shack. They put up the first life guard tower. It officially became Surfrider Beach.

Now, where there once were only ten guys surfing in September day, there were one-hundred kooks. My world was gone.

Valley Kooks: 4.
Malibu: 0.

It's 1994, we've entered round five. Malibu is the resin. I am the catalyst. Soon we'll be going off together. My world is going to come back. It will happen on my Aloha Wave.

The dead sixty-three year old man in the two-piece bikini laid stiffly in the water-filled bath tub. Little waves lapped over the porcelain round edges and splashed on the tiled floor. The floater was short. Well tanned. His skin cured to a rough leather from a life spent surfing in the sun. He was wide-shouldered, had a slight gut. He wore a woman's rubber-flowered bathing cap. His open eyes seemed bewildered, as if he never expected to drown in a pool of still water only three feet deep.

A note was in the adjoining room, among the driftwood sculptures, seashells, and bamboo furniture. The police didn't notice it at first. The kick-out missive was on a small piece of paper taped to a weathered balsa longboard. Surrounding the board were old photographs of well-developed young men and girls kicking back at the beach, or surfing on uncrowded six-foot waves at Malibu in 1948.

The alleged suicide note was simple:

Gidget must die

It was a small wire item in some newspapers across the country...

"The Gidget" Stunt Double Dies
Beach bum to surf entrepreneur
millionaire a suicide

Sun Valley—A California surfing legend who was a stunt double for the female lead in the 1959 film "The Gidget," was found dead yesterday in the bathtub of his ski chalet.

Billy "Buzzy" Stang, surf industry entrepreneur, 61, surfed for star Sally Gaines, who played The Gidget. He wore a bikini and bathing cap. With the surf industry boom created by the film, Stang and several of his surf buddies, along with "Gidget" author Francis Koolner, went on to make millions by founding Devine Foam, a patented urethane-based foam that made it possible to mass market surfboards.

The Source

Somewhere, a week ago, in waters sixteen thousand feet deep, during the Winter in the South Pacific...

A low pressure area of counter-clockwise swirling wind from an atmospheric storm dragged and pressed down on the ocean. This created ripples. These ripples offered more surface to the wind and turned into white caps. The white caps broke. Their energy became absorbed into a more turbulent sea. This energy swelled and stretched out through a flat apron of water and gradually converted from a choppy stretch of mountain ranges into miles and miles of smooth rolling hills separated by evenly spaced valleys that were as deep as the hills were high. These moving hills and valleys from the South marched at 120 west longitudinal degrees to the Summer in the North.

A small jutting beach in California faced toward the approaching South swell. Malibu's three perfectly positioned sand-covered rocky undersea points were splayed and waiting. The third point near the mouth of Malibu Creek. A second point, a few hundred yards to the right of it and nearer to shore. The first point, a few hundred yards from the second reef, and even closer to the beach.

The swell was still hundreds of miles away, but a noticeable act was happening. Within the rolling mounds of this swell was a darker hump of water, which somehow picked up more of the storm's core force. It was a much larger wave than any in the group. It grew at the expense of other waves and absorbed their power. It was going to be a monstrous wave. It would be the most massive comber to hit Malibu since 1955. A set wave of set waves.

Malibu lived for a dead South.

And Dead was coming.

Chapter two

Malibu AD. (After the Deluge): 1994. Fall.

The ocean was a foam omelet filled with kooks to the brooding surf legend, who sat on his leveled throne of sand at Malibu, an old balsa board beside him. He was fifty-five. He wore sunglasses, a large canvas hat lined with Indian feathers, a stained gray poncho, a seal tooth necklace, torn jeans, and huaraches. He was tan. The first light soaked a bloody crimson color into the sand around him. The slouched figure pulled an orange from a pouch pocket, and discreetly clutched the fruit with the stump formed by half of his left thumb. He expertly peeled the skin with his long, canary-yellow fingernails, which were discolored from working with explosives.

Surfer Joe scornfully looked through the smoggy haze at the melting orange sherbet sunrise. The turquoise waves wrapped around the outside underwater reef just off the point of land that jutted out near the Malibu Creek rivermouth. The third point reef bent the swell lines Southern direction and veered them in a parallel course to the shore. It made the clear blue ocean look like a moving furrowed field. The waves broke from left to right, and headed toward the Malibu pier. The tops of their ruler-edged walls were slightly overhead. It was clean. Joe remembered the huge swell in September of 1955 started like this. But, the waves were better in Joe's time. No kooks then. No condos and mansions entrenched in the hills. No sewage problems caused by untreated waste from The Valley flowing into Malibu through the creek. No crowds. No shortboards. No lifeguard tower. No young and tan trust funders playing volleyball. No overpriced bar restaurants like the Malibu Boardriders Club at the end of the pier. No surf contests every other weekend. Back in Joe's Malibu, there was one wave to a surfer. Now, there were hundreds on surfboards who paddled for any one of the six waves in a set that came through every five minutes. It broke down to sixteen kooks surfing on a wave meant for one. It was like a pile on. Their boards were only a few feet apart. No one could make a turn. As the wave came closer to shore, even more surfers paddled, jumped on it, and cut the other surfers off. Every one of these mental deficients traveled here to ride Malibu, and dammit, they were going to get their waves. The swarm sharply barked, yowled, and yelled. Some even blew *real* whistles they wore around their necks, but most grunted and swore at anyone they believed was in their way:

"Got it!"

"Hey! Hey! Hey!"

"My wave!"

"Behind you!"

"Don't stall."

"What the fuck are you doing?"

"Move asshole!"

The surfing kooks collided or intentionally ran into one other on turns. Boards flatly thudded, sharply cracked, or shot in the air. Kooks shoved each other off their sticks, or, tackled each other from behind. Others defensively dove underwater to avoid being hit by loose boards or planing surfers. The fallen and their victims yelled, shoved, splashed each other. And, as wave after wave rolled in, the crowd's behavior escalated, overlapped, and intensified. Those who collided on one wave, got the in way of surfers on the next wave behind it. And so on and so on. Regardless of the numerous collisions, the bulk of the confrontations rarely developed into fistfights. Most of the combatants indifferently resigned themselves to the lawlessness of the spot, threatened each other, then turned away and paddled out, ready to commit the same offenses again because everyone else was. And since the crowd was its own refuge, the same violators could keep coming there and never be held accountable for their repetitive behavior. It just didn't matter. In the fifties, Surfer Joe thought, Malibu was crowded, but it a crowd that knew each other. There were real locals. You had to pay dues.

You earned your spot in the lineup. You even had to earn the place you sat in the sand. There was a certain respect for a pecking order. Now, it was just a bunch of peckers. It was zoo-ed out with kooks. Surfer Joe despised kooks. They destroyed everything. Kooks. They ruined Malibu. She gave birth to them. She was the mother of all kooks. *She* did this. She...

"Gidg...Gidg...Gidg...," Joe sputtered, as if he were choking on the actual thought of her.

Joe suddenly found himself transported. He was surfing a wave that grew and darkened. Its crest threw the water in front of it. Joe was within a dark cylindrical tube of swirling water. The Black Tube. He was surfing. He crouched. The pitching canopy of water just barely over his head. Voices whispered and echoed within the tunnel's wet walls: "Gidget must die...Gidget must die...Gidget must die..." Joe heard the wet-slapping sound hitting of a board to a wave. He looked over his shoulder and caught a glimpse of a man's shadow surfing behind him. Stalking him. Gaining on him. Joe felt the figure was honing in for a kill shot.

"No!" Joe screeched, throwing up his hands to shield his face. The wave was gone. Joe sat in the sand, flailing at nothing.

"Yo, check it out, the bum's freaking," said a teenager. "Duh."

"Cool," said the other one. "Loooooser."

They laughed.

Joe glowered at the gawking duo. They had vapidly glazed eyes. Bright smiles. One had blonde hair hopelessly tangled in Rastafarian locks. He had silver zinc oxide on his nose. It gave the impression he was made of metal and his tanned colored paint had peeled off. The other, had a buzzcut, a nose ring. and skull tattoos. His face was coated with different colors of sunscreen that resembled war paint. They carried six-foot boards with painted flames on them. Shortboarders, thought Joe, arrogant nothings.

"Kooks," growled Joe, pronouncing the word with a twig-snapping k-sound and stretching the "oo" into a prolonged and very disgusted ooooo (as if it was something foul he stepped in). Joe finished the word off with a hard "k" and a hissy sizzled "s." He added, "Short boards, small minds, tiny dicks."

"Hey, chill dude," said the Rasta white guy.

"Uh, don't call me *dude*," tautly said Joe, menacingly. "That type of language increases my tension. You don't want to do that."

"Whatever," said the crewcut, shrugging and following his friend to the ocean.

"Yeah, I know. Life is short," Joe called after them. He clicked his cheek and tapped his sunglasses with his thumb and forefinger, muttering to himself. "*Your's* anyway."

Yes, Joe thought, in the old days those punks wouldn't have even got into the water. And if they did, he could shoot his board at them. Joe flashed to a memory.

"Slick," Joe reflexively spoke to his past.

The digital clock radio on the driftwood table beside Johnny Slickmeyer's water bed clicked to 5:30 a.m. and went off.

A news announcer said: "Yes, Buzzy Stang, Malibu surfing legend of the sixties, found a suicide. And the today's air quality is unacceptable...Now back to those two wacky guys on KWAVE!"

Slick hit the snooze alarm.

"Like what time is it?" pertly asked a sixteen-year old girl, reaching over and squeezing the forty-five year old man's package.

"Did you hear something about the sixties on the radio?" drowsily asked Slick, rubbing his straw blonde hair and his wrinkled teak-wood tanned face.

"Huh?" she asked with a blank expression.

"Nothing," said Slick, sitting up.

A gush of water flowed out from his nostrils.

"Gross," said the girl, giggling.

"It's the ocean in my head," said Slick. "I have water on the brain."

The blonde kept giggling. She rolled her tight and small-breasted body onto Slick's large chest. She had a nose ring in her left nostril and a tiny metal hook sticking out of her navel. The water bed sloshed and rolled underneath them. They stared at each other for a moment. She with curiosity. Slick with bewilderment-tinged apprehension. She ran her finger along the thin white line in the center of his tanned and creased forehead.

"You have this scar long?"

"Thirty years," said Slick, staring off. "I was fifteen."

"This is intense," said the blonde, smiling. "I totally thought like you were thirty to the max. I mean, when was that?" The girl clearly struggled to do the math.

"1964."

"I was like born in like 1978."

"An excellent vintage," said Slick, gently pushing her off him.

"God. I guess surfing keeps you in shape, huh?"

"Six-foot one and weigh one-hundred and eighty-five pounds, almost all muscle with a little fat," said Slick, slapping his slight gut. "But, the best meat has marbling in it."

She playfully rolled to the other side of the bed and looked at the bookshelf filled with neatly catalogued magazines. A label above the issues read: "Surfing World 1961 to 1967."

"How come these like only go to 1967?"

"*Like* that's when shortboarding came in and everything like turned into like shit."

"Concept!" she said, picking up a seashell-framed picture from the bookshelf. "My father surfs shortboards."

"He's a kook."

"That's tight."

"I don't care."

"Obvee."

"What?"

"It means obvious!" she said, slightly irritated. "I guess you're just too old to know that." She looked at the nameplate on the picture. "What's the Malibu Pit Crew? It's a rad picture."

She pointed to an eight-by-ten inch black-and-white photograph of the original Malibu Crew in 1957. There was Toobsteak, Kahuna, Surfer Joe, Flippy Weaver, Buzzy Devine, Crispy Johnson, Corky Barber, Grubby, and a ten-year old grem named Slick. The crew was in their prime. Mid-twenties. Tanned. Blonde hair all. Lanky builds. Dirty baggy white longish shorts. Some wore knee-length Navy peacoats. They sat in the sand. The Malibu Wall was in the background, surfboards angled against it.

"You were cute then. I mean you're still a hunk and all, I still would have got down to business with you," she said. "Looks like you guys had fun."

"It was perfect."

"What are those bumps on your knees?" she asked, looking deeply into the photograph.

"Surfer knots," said Slick. "From knee paddling we'd get those calcium deposits. Damn things saved my live. When I had to report for the draft, the army doc didn't know what they were. I told him I had a bone disease. I didn't have to go."

"To a war?"

Slick stared at her. He tried to remember how the night went. He saw the string bikini on the chair. A bottle of half-drunk tequila next to the pizza carton on the floor. Tequila. That explains this. Tequila—that was the mistake.

"Oh," he groaned, lying back down.

"What was all that noise about last night?" asked the girl.

"Oh, that was probably Crispy, he's a buddy of mine. I let him crash in the back yard. He doesn't have a home."

"No, not that," she said, lightly smacking his shoulder. "Like what happened to you in the middle of the night? You woke up in a cold sweat and went eightball. You were really vocal."

"I was in The Valley again," said Slick, closing his eyes. "I always have this dream where I'm trapped in The Valley with a day job, and have my board on my car and I'm trying to get to Malibu, and no matter what turn I make, I always keep finding myself back in The Valley."

"Intense."

"Yeah, I thought you'd take that revelation pretty hard," said Slick, opening his eyes. He rolled over, reached down, and felt underneath the bed. He knocked down an open and empty Vaseline jar. He found the phone, picked it up, and dialed.

"Who you calling this early?"

"I'm not calling anyone, I'm making the call," said Slick, motioning her to be silent. The phone at the other end of the line rang several times.

"Hello," said an uncertain voice, answering.

"It's Slick, how big is it?"

"That's a rather personal question, wouldn't you say?" said Skip Purpus, standing at the sidewalk phone stall along the Pacific Coast Highway by the Bu. An old longboard leaned against a three-foot high metal pole railing that ran along the sidewalk.

"Skip! I thought you'd never leave New Jersey," cheerfully said Slick, surprised. "You told me you were coming but I never thought—"

"Yeah," said Purpus, who was in his late thirties. He had an average build. Short and trimmed blonde hair. A slightly receding hairline. He was six-feet two. Had small love handles. He wore a baggy nylon swimsuit. He was pale.

"Man, I thought you had a day job. You know, getting fat, getting that office tan—all white and puffy. I just figured you'd die playing racquetball from a blood clot or something."

"Fuck that," said Purpus. "I've been paying into the system my whole life, supporting everyone else, so fuck it. It's my turn."

"No argument," said Slick. "Somebody's gotta do it. That's why you've always been my hero."

They laughed.

"So you just shined your job?"

"No, I have a sabbatical of six months."

"Sabbatical?"

"Yeah, I get paid six months to develop myself, I can work on my Malibu book and surf."

"They're paying you to surf?" asked Slick. "Score."

"Yeah, and I'm traveling real light. My car and an old beater longboard."

"You still have that Malibu Pig I left there from the sixties?" asked Slick, laughing.

"Your signature model, yeah," said Purpus, looking at the waves.

"You can crash here, I keep the key in the same spot."

"Thanks," said Purpus. "You going to be in that Gidget contest this weekend? There ought to be some good surfing in it."

"I don't do contests," said Slick with a slight edge.

"But it's all longboarding, the Beach Boys are even going to be there, and—"

"Hey, I'll see you out in the water," abruptly said Slick. "Oh, wait! I talked to those guys about giving you interviews. I told them you were cool."

"Yeah, okay," said Skip, taken aback by Slick's abruptness. "I'm doing a phoner on Corky, and going to see Flippy later today."

"I don't know why you want to write about the old Malibu, nobody really cares about Surfer Joe or me anymore."

"I had a mid-wife—er, life crisis," said Purpus. "I always wanted to write about Malibu. There's just always been something there for me. It's a search, what can I say?"

Slick affectionately said, "Hit it, bro."

"Tell you more later, I—"

"Oh, how big is the surf?" quickly said Slick, remembering why he called.

"Um, it looks like eight to ten feet."

"Eight to ten feet," doubtfully repeated Slick. "Are you sure?"

"Um," said Purpus, confused.

"Look at the surfers," patiently said Slick.

"Yeah."

"Now when they're riding the wave, is it above their knee, their shoulder, or their head?"

"Some are different," said Slick, not knowing the cool surfer phrase to use. "But most are up to their shoulder, and some are above their head when they get to the bottom of the wave but then it drops down to their shoulder."

"About four feet, shoulder to head high," said Slick. "Charge it, bro."

Skip hung up. Purpus felt awkward and stupid. He spotted an odd character walking up the sand toward him. The man wore sunglasses, a poncho, and an outlandish canvas hat that obscured his face. He carried a ten-foot wooden board.

"Hey, is that an old balsa board?" asked Purpus.

"Fuck you," said the man.

"Yeah it is a nice day isn't it?" said Purpus, smiling. He walked to the beach. The ten-foot long leash cord was wrapped around his ankle and connected to the board. He stepped on the loose cord, tripped, and fell in the sand.

"Kook," grunted the man, shaking his head and trudging away from Malibu.

Purpus stood up and walked toward the perfect surf. He wanted a taste of a Malibu wave. Sure, the time period was gone, but the wave that drew the surfers to the beach still existed. Skip could actually ride it and experience the same sensation. That seemed like a miracle. The grown man was eager and determined. His eyes wide open and clueless.

"Owwwwwwww," yipped Slick, hanging up the phone, bounding from the bed and putting on a swim suit. "Waves."

"Hey, are you saying you'd rather ride waves than me?" asked the blonde, who seemed amused more than offended.

"It's four feet," clipped Slick, walking into the small kitchen near the bed. "Maybe if it was two to three feet we might have something to discuss."

He opened the small refrigerator and took out an Anchor Steam Ale.

"You're drinking before you—"

Slick held his head over the dirty-dish filled sink and poured beer over his hair as he said, "They smell beer on you in the lineup, they fear you more."

Slick left the bungalow and went outside into the ice-plant covered yard. It was fifty-foot square, had a small shed for ding repairs, and was enclosed with a ten-foot wall of shrubbery, which had an opening arch for an entrance. A string hammock hung between two palm trees. He stepped over chunks of foam, broken board halves, abalone shells, resin-coated tongue-depressor sticks, mildewed template strips, various rubbing compound containers, tiny plastic catalyst bottles, aerosol-spray acetone cans, fiberglass remnants peeled from board repairs, discarded vodka and beer bottles, and several small butter tubs filled with hardened resin.

"You're going to bail without breakfast?" said the blonde, who came outside, topless, and jumped into the string hammock.

"It's okay, you don't have to cook me one," clipped Slick.

He walked beneath a ten-foot blue plastic ground cloth. It hung like an awning from the small bungalow. He went past a rack with shelves that held fifteen damaged surfboards in various states of repair. Fiberglass cloth hung from the noses and tails. Rails were taped off.

"What are you looking for?"

"My style," said Slick. "The Malibu Pig."

He pointed to an eleven-foot longboard, lovingly yellowed with age, dotted with inch-long smears that resembled fruit bruises. Slick's classic sixties stick was cradled within the rubber-cushioned u-shaped wooden slots of two four-foot high posts, which were supported by rusty car-wheel rim bases. The vintage board's deck had delaminated indentations where Slick kneepaddled, as well as curved dents over its tail, where he placed his weight to crank bottom turns. It had a large glassed-on wooden fin. The fiberglass along the sides had a slight green tint. Its cracked round nose was partially covered with silver duct tape. Slick picked up the thirty-five pound board, and held it sideways beneath his right armpit.

"Malibu Pig," said the girl. "Excuse me?"

"It was a board Kahuna designed and shaped, it was called the Malibu Pig," said Slick. "He was one of the guys in the picture. The rear of the board is wider than the tip—it's great for doing noserides. Slow and holds in there longer. The perfect board for a Malibu wave. It's too slow for most other waves. But for here, it's the perfect longboard." He smiled. "Don't you know your history?"

"What's 'No Surf Construction and Ding Repair?'"asked the

girl, pointing to the writing on the door of Slick's rusty green pick-up truck.

"Just a failed business," curtly said Slick, squeezing one of the girl's firm breasts and making a honking sound. "Later."

"Keep dreaming," the girl replied, watching Slick trot out through the shrub archway, and down a side road that connected to the coast highway and The Bu.

"Ooooooooooooowwwh," howled Slick, carrying his old surfboard and running to the ocean.

"You didn't howl like that last night!" she shouted.

"Concept!" he yelled back.

"Obvee," she added, smiling. She contentedly swung in the hammock, looked up at the sun through the rustling palm trees, and affectionately said, "Surfers."

From the Journal Of Surfer Joe

Surf is derived from the Latin word murmur. It's a sound source from our days being tucked within the embryonic juice of a curled over fallopian tube. It's the raw energy the doctor tried to spank out of us at birth. Nature's subconscious. It speaks to the ride. Surfing is a calling. When I'm locked into the curl, slightly crouched on my board and tucked deep in the hollow pocket, the white water throwing over my back, a curved and rising green shoulder sucks up in front of me. Then I enter another level, my board absorbs the flowing and propulsive juice from the sun and the moon and the earth and I become a tuning fork reverberating that ancient and primitive but soulful murmur. Surfing is more than religion. After all, Jesus walked on water but he never caught a wave.

Yes, my friends, that rising unbroken shoulder...it's an expectation of what you want the world to be, a perpetual and promising continuation opening up to you. Yes, the feeling of promise. And when you're riding your own wave, everything is always fresh. And the curl, the force that propels you forward but tries to tumble you over in its avalanche, that—that, is what the world is. A whole world of kooks trying to catch up to you, swipe you down into their boneyard, and bury your dream.

The wave is passion shaped by a point. You can't ride both sides. How many people commit to a ride to be somebody? They hesitate. They are one of the millions of dedicated nothings hugging the shore for the security of an even tan. No surf breaks in the mainstream. The best surfing is performed where you have the highest margin for success and an even greater odds for failure. Those who play it safe will hate you. Always. They had their chance, but instead, they paddled over or backed down from the wave you committed to. These kooks try to belittle your ride's significance. Some even lie to themselves and pretend they're riding it with possessions. They buy a house on the shore. Their home becomes a bunker. But within this shelter they can still hear your ocean dream in the empty shell of their unfulfilled lives. Kooks can't soundproof themselves from your exultation. They're haunted by the hoots of the men riding the only true wave: style.

"Uh, boss," said Surfer Joe, sitting behind the wheel of a South Pacific Phone Company van. It was stopped at the Hollister Ranch security gate.

"Huh?" dumbly said a guard in the booth. The gawky kid put down his Stephen King novel.

"Checking out the lines," said Joe, tapping his sunglasses.

"Sure there's no surfboard back there?" asked the guard, peering from the booth into the van's cab.

Joe expected the question. The Hollister Ranch was an affluent community of houses built on stretch of sand along the Pacific. It was South of Point Conception and had the most consistent surf breaks on the entire coastline. To Surfer Joe, Hollister represented the ultimate monument to kook supremacy. The Valley elite had established their kingdom. These guys didn't have the ability or the dedication to dominate a surf spot, so they simply bought one and ruled it through zoning and their money, and turned the place into an elite country club. The only way anyone could gain access to the beaches was through one secured road. You couldn't pass through the guard shack unless you were a property owner, or knew one of the homeowners. The only other option was to rent a boat, anchor a thousand feet off shore, and paddle into the break. But, that still didn't guarantee the rich locals would allow you to surf their perfect waves. Once you paddled out to their surf spot, the territorial kooks in the line-up simply circled to prevent you from catching a wave. Then, when you returned to your boat, you'd find someone had emptied out its gas canisters, and you came to shore. When you did, the security guards who probably ruined your boat, were the same guards who confiscated your board, and arrested you for trespassing. You couldn't win. It was their world.

"Uh, do I look like a surfer?" asked Joe, clicking his cheek.

The kid wiped the remains of a pastry from his mouth. He flatly stared at the man who was wearing a blue jumpsuit and blue cap. The guard hit a buzzer. The gate lifted.

Joe pulled the van away, and harshly whispered, "Kook."

Surfer Joe rode the narrow paved and curbed road. Every huge home he passed was well over a couple million. They all resembled two-storied, redwood side-shingled, domed space modules. Between the homes Joe saw miles of numerous point breaks with nicely peeling rights and lefts. No one was out. Yes, the Hollister Ranch waves were nice. But they were all the same to Joe, who viewed the break as completely predictable, manicured for the inadequate's ego. The rolling humps hit off a rock reef, bent, and peeled in the exact same spot. The predictable wave gave kooks the illusion they were making sections because of their surfing dexterity. It wasn't a ride that challenged you. It wasn't a wave you earned. It was a wave you purchased. The perfect kook wave.

Joe spotted the mailbox. It said "Corky Barber." Joe passed the driveway, pulled over near a phone pole and parked. He stood and wedged his way between the van's front seats and slid back the wire-grill panel partition. He went to the back of the van. Joe stepped over the rolled-up futon, and walked between empty cottage cheese tubs, cans of peaches, bags of oranges and soybeans. He ducked underneath the longboard hanging from the ceiling racks. He passed a wall of shelves which held a VCR and camera equipment. Joe bent down and picked up his journal from the floor. It was a large manuscript filled with drawings and photographs. He put it among several leather-bound classics on the bookshelf, which was just above a small TV screen. Joe went to a large closet by a tiny refrigerator in the far corner of the van's two rear doors. He slid back the closet door and shoved the hangered clothes to one side. He removed the back panel that concealed his private arsenal: a shotgun-shaped weapon called an M-79, an Uzi, a pistol, sticks of dynamite, numerous 40-millimeter shells and rounds of clips, several detonators, plastic primacord rope, clear bags filled with black-powder covered fuses, blasting caps, round rolls of green rubber-like datasheet explosive, and a water-filled plastic bucket that contained a sealed package of high-impact explosive called lead azite. Joe procured the weapons and the explosives through religious groups he met in his worldly travels. Joe was pleased, but he made one munitions miscalculation. He did have enough primacord and safety fuses to wire every Malibu structure, but Joe underestimated the fuses required for his extra curricular activities. He could easily buy safety fuses that would burn underwater and in moist areas, but the federales monitored those purchase, especially the type of quantity Joe needed. He didn't want to tip anyone off. So, Joe simply made thin fuses out of newspaper and covered them with a mixture of charcoal, sulfur, and saltpeter. These homemade fuses could be put out with water, but Joe figured with the other mix of explosives thrown in, it would all balance.

Just as Joe reached for the nine millimeter pistol, an internal throbbing pain rose and broke behind his ear. Its power dropped him. He fell backwards against the futon.

"Malibu," summoned Joe, wincing from the pain. "Malibu."

Joe needed to calm down. He laid on the floor, his head propped at an angle by the rolled futon. He closed his eyes and imagined himself back at Malibu. Before *her*. He saw Toobsteak's famous hut, which was roughly fifteen feet all around. The shack had palm-frond walls and a roof. It was supported by beams made out of telephone poles. A painted sign on the hut read "Locals Only." Balsa boards leaned against it. A small white picket fence ran around the place. The beach was completely deserted. Five-foot waves were wrapping around the point and peeling to shore. Only six surfers were out.

"Malibu," said Joe like an incantation.

Joe saw The Malibu Pit Crew. They were drinking beer, eating fish they caught, and munching vegetables they ripped off from a nearby rectory's garden. A beach bum named Seaweed waffled a chick in the shack. In the shorebreak, Lunchmeat, a four-hundred pound Samoan, wrestled with three cops who wanted to arrest him for some recent drunk and disorderly behavior, and probably a morals charge. A wasted Toobsteak was lying in the sand by an empty gin bottle. On his face, he wore a diving mask without the glass in it. A large sign beside him read: "Wake me up for lunch." Under the pier, amid a shower of curled wood shavings, Kahuna was taking a sharp drawknife to a ten-foot long by two-and-half foot wide plank constructed of glued-together white balsa strips. Near the shaper were two gremmies, trying to pull teeth out of a dead sea lion. The police couldn't get a grip on the slippery fat man in the water. Lunchmeat swam out to sea. The soaked cops trudged across the sand to their cars.

Joe fell asleep and dreamed...

Surfer Joe was dressed in swim trunks, barefoot, carrying a longboard under his left arm. He was seventeen-years old. Tanned. He walked on a sidewalk among commuters in suits who were hurrying to work. They walked one way and he walked in the opposite direction. They parted around Joe without acknowledging him. And then, the horde disappeared. Joe found himself intercut through numerous scenes that changed around him. He passed through wedding receptions, through maternity wards, and funerals. No one saw him. Joe went through living rooms of couples stuck at home because they had to watch their children. He ambled through aisles of a business offices while everyone worked at their desks. He sidestepped through partners at a Senior Center dinner dance. Finally, he was outside, walking down the center line of the Coast Highway. The jammed cars were bumper to bumper in both directions. He saw The Malibu. The shiny white crescent beach, palm trees, the pier, the shack, the tilted fragment of an old wall and the rusty wire fence angled from it to The Pit. Soon, he'd be surfing the waves. Surfing with the crew. Surfing.

Joe stood on the deserted beach. Where was everyone? The waves wrapped into the shore. But, the ocean wasn't making a sound. It was a sunny beautiful day, turning the gray Malibu Wall and the sand a bright white, as well as burning lighter shades of blue in the water. No one was in Toobsteak's shack. No one was fishing off the pier. There weren't any gulls or pelicans. Slowly, the white sand underneath Joe turned into a disturbing dim color. Joe felt as if the land were going to attack him, so he raced to the ocean, threw his board out in front of him, landed on it, and paddled to the outside third point. He turned around and straddled his board. The land was gone. There was only water. Joe looked back at the ocean. He saw a bulging, dark bluish, long bar of a rising hump. It made a sound, like a deep organ chord, a long sustained ominous one too. He stroked in front of the advancing hump, feeling it gently lift him. He stood and turned the board, trimming parallel across the wave. He rocked the board slightly, broke the fin loose. The board slid sideways down the turquoise slope. He stayed ahead of the whitewater, which looked like crumbling talus. The shore appeared again. The sand was gleaming white. Birds squawked. The ocean whomped and sizzled. Joe felt uncomfortable, as if a shadow was trying to overtake him. How could this be? No one was in the water. No one was on the beach. It was paradisiacal. But Joe still felt off. Then he glanced down. Under the water, alongside of his board. An object was locking in on him. It was a coffin. It was open. Lying inside it, with his arms folded across his tan chest was a dead surfer in swim trunks.

It was Joe.

"Nooooooooo!" he screamed from the board.

Suddenly, the glassy blue wave grew around him. Its curved face turned black. The top of the wave pitched and threw over Joe, as if it were a black tongue wrapping around him. The dark water drew Joe down into its gullet. And all Joe saw was blackness. There was no water. Just darkness. He was falling backwards into a pit. His longboard spun above him. He was going down, down, down. It kept getting blacker and blacker and blacker.

"Nooooooooooo!" screamed Joe.

He was yanked from the sea of his dreams and up through the surface of reality. He thrashed on his futon like a hooked fish in the bottom of the boat. His seal-tooth necklace chattered. Joe panted. His chest rapidly heaved. His bent sunglasses angled off his face. The sombrero hung behind his back from a strap around his neck. He caught his breath. He wiped his forehead, aligned his sunglasses, and put the hat back on. Then he reached into his poncho pocket and pulled out an old picture. It was a crumpled black-and-white photo of the Malibu Pit Crew on the set of "The Gidget" movie. The surfers stood in a group surrounded by the actors, the director, and the writer of the film. Most of them had felt-tip-drawn red circles around their faces and x's crossed within them. Joe looked for Corky.

"This is *my* movie now," said Joe, smirking as he drew a circle around the young director's face.

The Malibu Wave.

The Bu.

It happens every summer.

The unique Malibu wave is sculpted by these elements: a South swell, sand flow, wind direction, and underwater reefs. The three reefs are layered with thousands upon thousands of round but flat cobblestones, which are neither too small or too big—they're perfect to shape thin-walled waves. The rains from Winter storms flow out of the Malibu Creek estuary. These waters push out sand from the beach to the ocean. The flushed sand fills in the jagged cobblestone reefs, refining them into smooth, gradually descending slopes. This distinctive angled flooring of reefs delicately and slowly unzippers each bulging swell line. It chisels and sculpts a moving peak constructed of a pitching curl perfectly counterbalanced by a perpetually rising shoulder. The offshore winds glance across the wave's face, leaving markings resembling a heavily speckled silver glint, as if the wave's shoulder was a sheet of an unknown alloy being hammered, thinned, and curled up higher. Finally, as a breezy afterthought, a warm and windy brush stroke presses and flamboyantly combs back the turquoise wall's feathery tip into a mist laden with rainbows.

Most waves at other surf spots offer a short ride to a surfer. They peel for a while then section (which is when the wave closes out top-to-bottom) in front for a surfer. This closed-out section of foam washes out any chance of the surfer to trim across the swash and connect into the newly formed wave peeling down the line. That's why Malibu is so unique on a South. If you ride it right, it doesn't section. When the place is on and working it's better than any other summer surf spot. Everything about the wave is taut, vibrant, alive. Add a surfboard to it and The Malibu becomes perfect fun.

The Bu.

Johnny Slickmeyer kneepaddled on his longboard to get into a Malibu wave. He wasn't alone. He was surrounded by a flotilla of teenagers on shortboards who were competing for the same wave. They glared and sneered and frantically clawed into the slightly chilly water. The ocean's flat surface suddenly bulged and lifted Slick to its cream-tipped peak where the wave began to break. He looked down at the six-foot ledge that slanted below him to his right. Slick was in the perfect spot. It was his clearly his wave. But no one else saw it that way.

"Going right!" screamed a surf punk with blonde dreadlocks, who attempted to squeeze Slick out of the wave by paddling his shortboard under the man's eleven-foot stick.

Slick sprung up and quickly swung his board around to the left, grazing the teenager's dangling locks.

"Fucking Valley!" screamed the kid, jumping backwards and using his feet to shoot the pointed shortboard at Slick, who ducked, tumbled, and did a face plant on his board's deck. The curl alongside swamped him. Slick held onto his stick and went over the crashing falls.

Slick surfaced, enraged, and grumbled, "I got my hair *wet!*"

A seething Slick grimly paddled back to the line up, and positioned himself next to the dreadlocked teenager.

"Give me your stick dog face," Slick barked, splashing the punk with water.

Rasta Head indifferently stared at the next approaching set. His arms were folded across his tan chest. His legs straddled a chip-shaped shortboard. He was sunk up to his armpits.

"You're real tough when you're on a wave and you can use your board as a weapon," said Slick, splashing water in the kid's face. "But when you're floating on your stick, looking a man in the eye, you talk the talk but can't walk the walk." Slick smacked the water and splashed the kid again. "Who you are is your problem, *what* you are is mine. Now, give me your fucking board, you limp-dick, disco-hip jiggling kook."

"Get out of here, you fucking troll," truculently snarled the dreadlock-waggling punk.

"Troll!" bellowed Slick, infuriated. "I surfed this place before you were born. You fucking valley piece of shit!"

Slick shoved the kid into the water. He flipped the punk's shortboard over. With the flat part of his palm, Slick cleanly punched out the center fin, and the two smaller side fins. He grabbed the terrified kid by his dreadlocks and pounded his head against the "One love" decal on the shortboard's bottom.

"Let him go, old fart," shouted the punk's buzzcut amigo.

"I'm not *done* with him yet," said Slick, slamming the kid down one more time and letting him go. "Jah."

"You didn't have to do this," mewlishly said Rasta Head, looking at the damaged tail.

Slick narrowed his eyes and firmly said, "No I didn't, but I don't think you'll *ever* try to snake me again, will you?"

"Outside!" someone shouted.

An approaching purplish bulge emerged from the ocean as it formed around the underwater reef.

"Old fart coming through," Slick announced, kneepaddling for the wave. No one near him went.

The flat water rose into a reassuring steep cliff, lifting Slick to its high precipice. Slick felt a force beside his own move him forward. He slid down the rising wave, angling to the left, slowly standing up, and smoothly bringing the board around to the right in one flowing motion. A sweep of spray fanned out from its tail. He straightened the longboard into a parallel position across the shoulder. Slick stood with his knees slightly bent. He rode in the curved pocket just ahead of the spilling crest behind him. Cool foam splattered on his muscular back. Slick deftly pressed his foot on the board's inside rail. The board quickly rose and trimmed just below the wave's feathered tip.

Ahead of Slick, the wave's shoulder-high sheer cliff tapered down into a smaller liquid dune with a pinched-tip slope. Slick cross stepped back, placed his rear foot on the tail, bent his knee and cutback into the curl of salt-water lather. This move gave the wave a chance to reform a steeper shoulder in front of him again. As the wave moved closer to the shore, it hollowed out with a curved inward face and broke faster. Slick drove his cutback deeper and deeper to the flatter part of the wave behind the curl. The half-cylindrical shoulder stretched out longer. Its curved face looked like a low-slung six-foot high and twenty-foot long vertical sail. The whole section was just on the verge of closing out. Slick arched his back, gracefully swung a bottom turn, and brought up his board to the right. His Malibu Pig screamed down the line. He took six quick cross steps to the tip. The descending pressure from the breaking wave on the tail enabled Slick to keep all his weight on the front of the board without tilting and sinking it. He wrapped his ten scarred toes over the edge of longboard's nose. Slick assumed an indolent but casually defiant stance, slightly pushing his hips forward, throwing back his shoulders, and keeping his arms down at his side. The thinned out wall became more luminous from the sunlight and blended into the bluish sky. The curl's foam slathered over the board. And, for several gloriously immune seconds, Slick was perched and holding. A Toe God on the frontal edge of his parallel universe, indifferently standing on a low puffy cloud cruising across the sky.

"'The Gidget' was written by Koolner, who was The Gidget's stepfather, and when he heard about the surfers and their luaus he thought it'd make a good book," said Corky Barber, talking to the speaker phone placed atop the driftwood end table. "It was a story of a teenage girl who befriends surf bums and falls in love with Surfer Joe. She gave Joe his nickname too."

Corky sat on a thick cushioned bamboo chair in his sunken living room, looking through his bay window at the clean waves peeling off the reef break in front of his estate. Corky was no longer the young man Joe circled in the Malibu Pit Crew picture. His once luxurious blonde hair was still blonde but thinned and methodically raked out across his scalp, resembling eel grass clinging to a rock. His sun-cracked skin was rough but tanned. His teeth were yellowed, and jagged like a rocky jetty. His throat seemed dried out, two curved veins extended over the vocal cords. He looked like a leather frog with a bad toupee.

"Anyway, The Gidget," continued Corky to the speaker, "who I'm certain you know was Sally Koolner, a stepdaughter from one of Koolner's many marriages. Anyway, she became a successful realtor—I'm certain her father's money helped her, but don't quote that. Koolner and Buzzy made millions when they founded Devine foam. Kahuna cleaned up by mass marketing boards. Flippy made a pretty healthy chunk of change from 'Surfing World' magazine. Toobsteak capitalized on any part of it, or used his name to make money. He works at the Malibu Surf Museum and tells stories. I made my money with surf films and bad beach movies. And Surfer Joe? He ended up with an image no one cared about anymore."

"Slick—" said the speaker phone voice.

"There's a guy who is bitter," interrupted Corky. "He got burned by Joe more than anyone. Slick never got the recognition he deserved. But he could never market himself. You know who was really hot? Who Joe copied? You ever see Crispy Johnson? Now, he's a character from the old school. Crispy stopped surfing when a couple valleys came out on a weekday and burned him on his wave. If that was the future he wanted no part of it. That guy, if you see old pictures of him, you'll see where Surfer Joe got his stances and gestures." He shook his head. "Crispy's a drunk now."

"Wasn't there an incident where Joe lost his—"

"The explosion at Grubby's, you mean," said Corky, almost too quickly, which he sensed. Corky slowed down to smooth the moment over. "Shit, surf shops are notorious for fires. Vaporized acetone. You know what that is? Ever breath that shit? The place just went. People can think what they want."

"What do they think?"

"How so?" warily asked Corky.

"Well, it seemed—"

The chimes at Corky's front door rang out the beginning notes of a Beach Boy's tune called "Surfing USA."

"Look can you get back to me in a few minutes?" asked Corky, who seemed eager to end the conversation at the mention of the surf shop explosion. "I have someone at the door."

Surfer Joe quickly pulled his finger away with revulsion, recoiling at the doorbell's Beach Boys tune.

"Beach Boys," said Joe to himself. "Man, I hate the fucking Beach Boys! Stealing the culture of my world." Joe mockingly sang, "Fun fun fun in the sun sun sun, grab a girl and bring your woody to the beach. Surf surf surf." Joe seethed with repugnance. "The Beach Boys! Kooks with amplifiers. Had to let the secret out. They couldn't keep their goddamn mouths shut! They had to tell everybody in the whole frigging world about surfing. Best thing that ever happened to Western Civilization is Brian Wilson was never able to complete that *Smile* album. The Beach Boys! They didn't even surf. They never surfed. And the one who said he surfed, *drowned*. Gives you an idea of how good a surfer he was."

Joe imitated a water-gurgling sound of a man drowning and sang, "Help me Rhonda"

The Malibu Wall.

To a kook The Wall is a graffiti-covered eyesore of grayish bricks. A dangerous and useless structure that should be torn down instead of supported by metal braces along most of its length. That's how a kook would see it. But to those with a clue, the crumbling and cracked wall was a fortification left from an historic but lost battle. The Wall commemorates a place, a period. It's the birthstone of modern surfing. What Cooperstown is to baseball, Malibu is to surfing. In the twenties and the thirties, surfboards were blunt-shaped planks that weighed over one hundred pounds. Malibu's perfectly peeling waves were the ultimate laboratory to work on board design. In the beginning, boards were so primitive, surfers didn't angle across the wave, they merely took off and went straight to the shore. Throughout the thirties, forties, and fifties, Tom Blake, Bob Simmons, Joe Quigg, Dale Velzy, Dave Sweet, and Hap Jacobs, worked on different shapes, fin designs, and materials to improve the surfboard's maneuverability. For those detail mongers, Blake was credited as the first designer to put a fin in the board, Simmons was given credit for giving them planing speed, and Velzy and Jacobs modified them further to make them really turn.

The Malibu Wall is all that remains of an adobe-style brick barricade that once protected the Rindge estate. Its height varies with the amount of sand that's built up against it, but The Wall is about twelve-feet high, and it's roughly three hundred yards from the ocean and runs at a slightly northern angle away from the shore. The thousand-foot long cracked and tilted wall extends from the only building left from the Rindge legacy, the old Adamson estate house, a Spanish-Moorish place by the mouth of the Malibu Creek estuary. It's a museum for Chumash artifacts and Malibu history, but it also houses—rent free—a kook who is a state college education official. Outside of the estate house, The Wall is the last remnant from the turn-of-the-century days of the Rindge ranch. A flat reddish orange brick trim runs across The Wall's terraced top. Placed every twenty feet along it are squat, red-tiled, three-foot high turrets. The Wall's grayish blocks are juttingly interspersed with brittle-like clusters of extended red bricks, round stones, or cobbled patches of brightly colored patterns of ceramics (which were from Rindge's old tile company). The Wall's only arched opening leads from the beach to a small parking lot that's twenty feet below the level of the Pacific Coast Highway. On the beach side, just a short distance to the right of The Wall's archway entrance—where Toobsteak's old palm-frond shack once stood—is a square grayish-brown brick building that houses municipal bathrooms and showers (facetiously referred to by locals as the Toobsteak Memorial). And further down from the bathroom is a lifeguard wooden tower. At the Wall's jagged end, is an eight-foot high chain-linked fence that runs for a hundred feet with barb wire along its top. This fence is part of a square that encloses a sandy-covered asphalt area for the storage of yellow garbage drums and state vehicles. It's strewn with shattered glass and rusted tin cans.

Some surfers find a reverential assurance in The Wall's dingy grandeur. They view it more like the iconic ruins of an oracle on consecrated ground. This seemingly insignificant wall is their altar to surfing. It's a place where their one particular message must constantly be written and seen by the kook world. The message represents a mythical figure far larger than the real person. The underlying meaning of the message declares that no matter what burdens or tasks the world throws on an individual, a surfer's spirit is always just ahead of it, styling and free. Every other day, park officials sandblast the sect's scripture off The Wall. But, no matter how many times the county erases the words, the next day, some tweaked mendicant returns and repaints them.

Slick enviously stared at the handwriting on The Wall:

Surfer Joe Lives.

The red painted letters dripped at their edges, as if the Malibu Wall was bleeding from a fresh wound.

"What bullshit," grumbled Slick.

The kooks felt Joe represented the surfer spirit, but Slick knew Joe only represented himself. The kooks didn't see it. Joe treated kooks with contempt, but they identified with Surfer Joe because the kooks wanted to see themselves as rebels. Sure, Joe preached about his Malibu waves, and how no kook had a right to burn him by dropping in front of him. Yeah, but he thought nothing of taking off in front of you, fading his board toward you, and driving you back into the foam. The curl would break between you and Joe, allowing him to steal your wave because you couldn't make the section. But if *you* burned Joe, he would either run over you, shove you off your board, or shoot his board at your head. Once an Joe-awed kook became Joe's victim in the water, the legendary aura was gone, and the enlightened kook realized what Joe was. But to everyone else, and there were legions of everyone else, Surfer Joe was the legend, the true surfer, the one who had the best time period to surf Malibu, and who rode Malibu better than anyone else. He was the resentful rebel who had his surfing paradise ruined by commercialism of his private lifestyle. Yes, Surfer Joe, the legend who surfed all over the world and never held a real job. The kooks believed it, and Joe counted on it, the whole Surfer Joe myth was part of his hustle. The myth allowed him to borrow money and not repay it, get treated for free meals and drinks, bum rides, and be given cheap rents or housesitting assignments from the rich. And what did Joe give back to his benefactors? Nothing. They were kooks and deserved to be taken. He owed them nothing.

"There's only *one* King Of Malibu," Slick scornfully said. He disapprovingly snorted like a bull. "Huh."

Slick shrugged. He leaned the waxed side of his battered board at an angle to The Wall and laid his towel in the sand below the writing. He sat against The Wall. Slick enjoyed pressing his back on the warm but rough bricks. He closed his eyes and felt the sun's glowing intensity lightly roast away the cool beads of water on his chest and dry his sun-bleached hair. Two orange sunspots burned through his lids, as if someone with an acetylene torch was trying to break into his skull. Slick's veins still pulsed out the stoke he absorbed from surfing. The sand seemed to leech out his impurities. He deeply inhaled the salt air and the aroma of seaweed and sun tan oil. Slick listened to the Malibu waves crumple and effervescently fizzle on the shore and the ou-ou squawking of seagulls. A slight warm breeze brushed along the outline of his body, curving upwards, licking around his limbs like flames. Slowly, he slipped into a trance where the sounds of the present mingled with sharp and rapidly flitting fragments of memories, the shifting texture of half-remember dreams, and floating undeveloped thoughts. He surfed it.

"Slick, don't you ever work?" asked a familiar and very unwelcomed denture-whistling voice.

This particular human eclipsed Slick's sun buzz. Slick was pulled back into the world of screeching beachgoers, the thump and smack of volleyball players, loud radios, and kooks yadda-yada-ing about film or sales deals on cellular phones. A drugged grogginess clung to him like syrup. He felt cranky.

"What are you, a cop?" grunted Slick, scowling.

It was Francis Koolner. Not only did no one like him, no one even liked *looking* at him. Koolner was in his mid-seventies. An aneurysm of a man. He was short and nearly muscled. His smooth skin was so pale he always looked like he was recovering from a recent stroke. He had a grayish mustache, a pot belly, skinny legs and arms, and a vulture-like wattled throat. He wore a sailors cap, thick prescription wrap-around sunglasses, red knickers, as well as a freshly pressed yellow Malibu Golf Club shirt. A small black box with a rubber antenna was tucked under his armpit.

"And don't even bother asking me to surf in your goddamn Gidget contest this weekend," growled Slick. "I don't do contests."

"Don't even bring that up," said Koolner, groaning. "A whole bunch of protesters are going to be surfing in the water that day, anyway. They found out the contest permit just means we have the right to the beach but not the exclusive use of the ocean."

"Good, it's nice to know there are some things even cheesedicks like you can't own," said Slick, spitting in the sand. "Because of the shit from your treatment plant and condominiums you built up in the hills, I almost got hepatitis last year."

"Should have worn a condom," cheerfully said Koolner, who loved personal confrontations. He gazed at the ocean. "The waves looked kinda fun yesterday."

"I couldn't make it yesterday, I was taping," replied Slick.

"A movie?" asked Koolner, leaning back to convey surprise.

"No, drywall."

"Here I was thinking you were finally catching onto the game," said the old man, shaking his head.

"Well, we all make mistakes, how about your waterslide project in Bakersfield?"

"What a fucked idea that was," said Koolner, snorting. "Putting a slide in Bakersfield. Christ, Bakersfield is the lowest point on the planet, you can't slide any further down than that."

"Sounds like a good place for you to live," said Slick, pleased with himself.

A group of children screamed nearby.

Koolner turned toward the distant commotion and shouted, "Stinkers! Stinkers!" Near the water's edge, a large brown-and-black mottled dog chased children, terrifying them. Koolner's heavily veined right hand quickly grabbed the black box from under his armpit. He hit a switch to turn it on. Then he pressed a button. It sent an electric shock into the dog's collar. The four-legged ogre suddenly yelped and jumped.

"Nice, I wish I had one of those in my last marriage," noted Slick, laughing. "Probably for me."

"Stinkers!" commanded the old man.

The dog came to its master and sat at his feet. The mongrel had mean eyes and a muzzle dripping with saliva. The low-life fleas in the sand quickly bounced away, as if even they wanted no part of this animal.

"What kinda breed is that?"

"It's a Rotweiller and German Shepherd."

"So it's a Rotten-shepherd," said Slick, smiling.

"Surfer Joe is back at the Bu," grimly said Koolner, looking off at the ocean. Slick stopped smiling. "Really."

"Joe's been gone for twenty five years," said Slick. He stared the old man's huge sunglasses. They reflected 'Surfer Joe Lives.'

"He's come back to kill everyone involved in The Gidget movie for ruining Malibu."

"Concept." said Slick, delighted.

"Yes, my friend," softly said Joe, twitching his cheek as he took off his hat. He smiled with a significant gap between his two front teeth. "Time to get happy."

Corky studied the sun-bleached haired man on the front door steps. He wore sunglasses, a poncho, shorts, sandals, and a necklace made of sea lion teeth. The odd man held a slightly ripped canvas hat lined with feathers and Indian beads. The six-foot surfer crouched slightly, hunched his shoulders, leaned back on his right foot and extended his left, as if he were hanging five toes on the nose. The stranger took off his sunglasses and Corky clearly saw the familiar blue eyes set within the deeply tanned and wrinkled face.

"Joe! You look great, bro," said Corky, who wanted to hug his old friend, but held back.

"Fifty five. Uh, delaminating a little at the edges of time," answered Joe, clicking his cheek and adjusting his sunglasses. "You know me, never an honest day in my life's work."

"Come on," said Corky, waving Joe in.

They stepped down into the sunken living room with its vaulted ceiling. The place was decorated with a beachcomber motif. Bamboo chairs. Glass-topped tables with shells. The white-bleached wooden walls adorned with posters of numerous surf movies as well as black-and-white photographs of the old Malibu days. In the corner was a weathered balsa longboard.

Corky pointed to the peeling waves that broke in front of his house and said, "That's where I spend my retirement. Surfing. No crowds."

"Nice retirement home," said Joe, looking at the ocean. "Dig, you work your ass off your whole life just so you can have enough money to afford the same lifestyle you had when you were broke." He clicked his cheek and tilted his head. "Crazy, man." He tapped his sunglasses. "If you never made that film, you wouldn't need all this."

"Yeah, right," snorted Corky. "Hey, what happened to Malibu would have happened anyway."

"It's too bad you never gave me the option to see if it would have been true otherwise," Joe said in an uncompromising tone. "All I wanted to do was just surf. You took that away."

"Because of The Gidget movie?"

"Gidg...Gidg,...Gidg," sputtered Surfer Joe.

A throb of pain spread and created a brain wave that swelled inside Joe's head. It pitched and threw. Joe was back surfing within the Black Tube. The swirling dark walls encircled him. The voices reverberated around the narrowing tunnel: "Gidget must die, Gidget must die, Gidget must die." There was splashing behind him again. The sound of a board being slapped down on the water to gain speed. Joe saw the shadow of a surfer.

"The Gidget?" said Corky.

"Yes!" Joe snapped, suddenly shivering. The Black Tube was gone.

"Well, those days were good days," warbled Corky, unsuccessfully trying to act casual. "But things change."

"It's the curse of the Chumash," gibbered Joe, speaking very softly as if he were talking to himself. He adjusted his sunglasses. "It's the curse. Think of it. Kooks took away the Malibu, and now the Valley pollution is killing them. It's the curse don't you see? We destroyed the Malibu and now the Malibu is destroying us." He paused. "I can still feel the angry stares of the Chumash on my back." He tilted his head. "I listen to them."

"Really," said Corky, cautiously taking a step back from Surfer Joe.

Corky was surprised Surfer Joe still conversed in the self-possessed tone of a fifties hipster. Joe had the same animated quirks—the twitching shoulders, the rapidly darting hand movements that jabbed the air, the cheek clicking, the tilting of the head to emphasize a point, and the way he constantly adjusted his glasses with his right thumb and forefinger. But, it just didn't flow. Now, there was a warble to the image. His crow's feet resembled stress cracks. The gestures which were once spontaneous and casual, now seemed forced, jagged, and harshly eccentric. There was no self-conscious humor. He sounded spooked, and distrustful. The playful hand movements seemed slightly paranoid, as if they were clawing motions to protect himself from an invisible foe. It was as if his own persona, the soul surfer, had devoured him.

"Run into any of the old Pit Crew?" uneasily asked Corky.

"Uh, you could say Buzzy and I spent some time in the water together," casually said Joe, spotting film canisters on a nearby table.

"How is he?"

"At peace with himself," quipped Joe, going to the table and opening a canister. "Hey, is that a print of *the* film?"

"Yeah," nervously said Corky. "Koolner's going to show it at a party after the contest. It's at the Malibu Boardriders club. You know, the one at the end of the pier. Nice place, glass windows look out at the Bu. You can sit there, have a brew, and watch the surfers. The Beach Boys are going to show up too. Kahuna is making them some new kind of surfboard. You ought to come by..."

The phone rang.

"You want to get that?" asked Joe, pointing his half thumb at the ringing object.

"Yes," quickly said Corky, turning his back on Joe. "What do you think of the view I have of the ocean?"

The phone rang.

"Killer," answered Joe, wrapping several strands of movie film in a tightening noose around Corky's frail throat. Joe whispered in an almost loving coo, "Surf's up!"

The Valley.

The Valley is a rusty orange smog. You can easily get misled in its haze. It will make you flail, stumble, trip, grope. You can't find its pulse or your own. You don't know who you are or what you want anymore. It's a confusing place teeming with sticky asphalt and hot concrete and sharp-gleaming glass and angry traffic lights. It's a maze, a trap, a swamp, a comfortable first marriage without love. It's screeching metal, gunshots, endless stretches of brake lights, clogged overpasses, jack-knifed tractor trailers, stalls, and grime. It's tension, stress, pressure, sewage-line assessments, and a promotion without a raise. It makes you gain weight in your butt, makes you weak, makes you lose your tan, hair, and passion. It makes you look back but never ahead. It makes you sigh and drink and stare off. It twists you. It makes you criticize people you never met, get in arguments about topics that don't matter to you. It takes you away from yourself and deludes you into thinking it's fine, and by the time you realize The Valley deluded you, used you, drained you—well, by then, and, unless this insight happens to you at an early age, you're too weak to escape it. You're a dying man, adrift on the land away from the ocean, away from the surf, fading away from your style, away from your shoreline.

You died in pursuit of a false stoke.

"Are you trying to tell me Surfer Joe is going to kill everyone in 'The Gidget' movie?" asked Slick, highly amused.

"I'm not telling you he's going to kill everyone in 'The Gidget'," replied Koolner. "I'm telling you he *is* killing everyone in 'The Gidget' movie." He paused. "And he wants to kill me too."

"Obvee," said Slick, smiling. "I'm surprised he didn't start with you."

"Hey, this isn't a joke, look at this," said Koolner, reaching into his jacket pocket for a letter and handing it to Slick, who looked down at the paper. Suddenly, a spurt of sea water came out of his nostrils and landed on the page.

"The ocean, stays in my head for days," Slick said, shaking out the paper to dry it off.

"Probably just all the moisture inside such a dark hollow place," said Koolner, smiling.

Slick ignored the old man and read the circled portion of the letter from the film company's public relations department:

> This letter is in response to your inquiry for the names and addresses of the actors who took part in the film "The Gidget," which was released by our studio in 1959. Unfortunately, although the film was only released in the late fifties, all the cast members are deceased.

"Who cares, they were shitty actors," gruffly said Slick.

"He even knocked off the 'The Four Sophomores!'" said Koolner. "They did 'The Gidget Goes to Malibu' theme song, and 'Surf with Me My Love.' I always liked that one. You know, 'Surf with me my love, surf with me my love.'" Koolner sang the song, held his right arm up, and his left arm out, and smoothly danced with an invisible partner.

"You don't care about anybody," said Slick, smirking.

"Joe's not going after the actors anymore," said Koolner, twirling around in on spot, and stopping his dance with an arm flourish. The old man paused. "He killed Buzzy."

"What?"

"It's only on today's front page," said Koolner, flicking Slick the newspaper. "You'd never see it because it's not in a tide book."

"Buzzy, he was just a little before my time. But, he let me ride his board," said Slick, scanning the article. He shrugged. "Why do you need me? I'm just a nail banger who does ding repair. I mean, how hard can it be to find a fifty-five year old surfer with a gap between his teeth and a missing part of his left thumb?"

"On this beach he'd blend right in," said Koolner, pointing at several unshaven and uncombed surfers wearing dingy clothes.

"It's because of Grubby isn't it?"

"I didn't mention Grubby and you didn't mention him either," firmly said Koolner. "Look, the cops won't see the motive unless I show it to them. They don't know the surf scene. But you know this place. Everyone respects you. Any surfer from the old days hates me. Watch."

Koolner took a few steps toward Crispy Johnson, who was rummaging through a yellow trash drum. Crispy pulled out a few deposit bottles. The whiskered man was in his mid sixties. He had short grayish hair that looked like a coating of salt. Crispy's complexion was more of a reddish-blue bruise. He wore a rumpled swimsuit and a soiled "Windandsea" silver jacket. He was shirtless.

"So, Crispy, how's it going?"

"Blow me, Koolner."

"See, he hates me," triumphantly said Koolner, smiling.

"Hey Slick, hot tip ride," shouted Crispy, smiling. His yellow teeth were gray limned and coated with red-wine stains. Crispy shook liquid out of a can. "Saw that shortboarder shoot his stick at you." He laughed; it turned into a cough. "That kook made you do the dance of the flamed-out takeoff."

"It's a little hairy out there," said Slick, flicking a sand flea off his leg and onto the dog.

"Sorry to interrupt this intellectual round table discussion, but I have a proposal," said Koolner. "We're going to demo a new modern longboard at the contest. Kahuna is shaping them. Longboarding is going to be big. A lot of guys raised their families and are coming back to surfing."

"Gez, and I missed them so much," said Slick.

"You can get in on the ground floor," said Koolner, smiling. "What do you say?"

Slick removed a small rubber squeeze bulb from he folds of his towel. He stuck the blue bulb's point into his right ear, he compressed it, and sucked out the water accumulated in his canal. He squirted the bulb's contents on Koolner's shirt.

"Stinkers, protect!" shouted Koolner.

The Rotweiller-Shepherd growled and sprung upon the surfer. Its jaws struggled against the muzzle. Saliva dripped onto Slick's face.

"Get your fucking dog off me," said Slick, pinned by the mongrel.

"Back Stinkers," said Koolner, laughing. The dog didn't respond. "Stinkers back!" barked Koolner, hitting the button. The dog yipped from its collar's electric shock. Stinkers obediently returned to its master's side.

"You're an asshole," said Slick, wiping the sand off himself, and sitting up.

"Stinkers loves his Daddy," tenderly added Koolner, petting the animal, who seemed more terrified of the owner's affection than his punishment.

"Yeah, he just glows in your presence," said Slick.

Koolner tossed a bankroll of bills in Slick's lap. All Slick saw were hundreds.

"That's two thousand bucks," said Koolner. "That'll keep you in beer and waves for awhile."

Slick flicked the bills back to Koolner.

"I've gotten this far in life without your money, why do you think I'd take it now?"

"Something bothers you about me doesn't it?"

"Yeah, but the term 'something' isn't broad enough—"

"Let me guess what it is. Is it your lack of success compared to mine?"

"No."

"Damn, I thought that was it," said Koolner, loudly snapping his fingers. "You think a surf bum like Surfer Joe is worth something? After what he—"

"You going to chop off my finger if I don't do it?"

"It's not like you owe the guy anything, Slick"

"It's not my wave, I don't want it—"

"You wouldn't be here talking to me if Surfer Joe didn't take *your* wave away..."

Slick rubbed the whitish scar tissue in the middle of his tanned forehead...

Thirty years ago...

It was in the first heat of the Malibu Classic Invitational. Slick and Surfer Joe took off on the same wave. It was Slick's wave. But Surfer Joe dropped in front of him. Without any hesitation, Joe turned left toward Slick. The board knifed around like a scythe. Its edge solidly cleaved a six-inch gash in the middle of Slick's forehead. Joe kept turning, let the wave set up, and ruthlessly hung ten.

Awhile later, Slick regained consciousness. His head throbbed. The salty taste of blood came from his throat. He was lying in the sand. He sat up. The dazed Slick blearily watched Surfer Joe surfing in the finals.

"You were ripped off Slick," said Crispy, standing over his friend, drinking a beer concealed in a paper bag. "Joe did a flyaway on you and took you out. He has the name, so, they even ruled that you interfered with his wave because he was up first. That was your wave."

"Nice," said Slick, lightly touching the bandage on his head.

"Look at him," said Johnson.

The wave in front of Joe sectioned, breaking before him. Joe slid his board just underneath the white water. He took a step, did a slight arch, placed the left hand on his stomach, and held his right hand up, as if he were taking an oath.

"That's not even his style," said Slick. "He got that style from you, Kivlin, and Quigg."

"He can't steal me," said Crispy, belching. "That *is* me."

"Well, he's stealing something."

"I feel sorry for him, Slick. Imagine winning this contest and knowing that you don't really deserve it. That's a man who is in pain, Slick. He's in real pain."

"No, I'm in real pain," said Slick, gingerly probing the bandages on his head. He winced and laughed.

"No reason you should be sucking that guy's hind tit," said Crispy, hawking mucous up from his throat and adding, "Man, I hate winners."

"Wake me up when it's over," said Slick, lying back down on the beach. "There is a crowd. There are cameras. Joe'll get into a surf magazine. A legend is born..." He passed out.

Two hours later, Slick awoke. A stench filled his nostrils. He bolted up, urine dripping from his face.

"There's only one King Of Malibu," said Joe, zipping up and walking away with his trophy.

"Slick, you would have been considered the hottest surfer who ever rode this place," said Koolner. "But, instead, Surfer Joe's a legend. And you're an insignificant beach bum, I'd be a little bitter about that."

"Concept," said Slick, studying the sand he was squeezing out of his fist. "Look, it's between you guys. I could care less. Besides, I never get into arguments about other guys' waves."

"You're on this wave whether you want to or not, Slick," said Koolner, walking away.

"Are you saying I'll end up like Grubby?" challenged Slick.

Koolner turned, his eyes narrowed, and he said, "That can happen to anyone." His gaze lingered over Slick. Koolner kept going.

Slick watched the old man stroll along the beach. His dog Stinkers scared even more children and chased after seagulls. The guy made his fortune ruining this place, mused Slick. Nothing touched Koolner. Hell, Koolner even paid off the lifeguards so he could walk his Rotten-Shepherd on the beach. Nothing touched Koolner except Joe. The old man still feared Joe. So there was hope.

The breeze lifted up the newspaper, Slick caught it against his leg. He looked at its second page. A story drew his interest:

Malibu incorporates in self-rule move

Topanga—Malibu, which represents the California dream and lifestyle, is an open sewer.

Malibu officials voted to incorporate the county into a town to avoid a federal mandate requiring residents to raise funds to build their own multi-million dollar sewage treatment plant.

"The millionaires in the most exclusive real estate area in the country, are allowing their own children to swim in their own waste," said Ken Dixon, Department of Environmental Protection spokesman.

Over the years, Malibu has been plagued by untreated sewage. Increasing numbers of surfers at Malibu have contracted hepatitis, stapf, ear infections, and, in two cases, surfers needed heart transplants due to Coxsackie B-4 virus.

"I think it's a major victory for us," said Francis Koolner, president of the Malibu Preservation Society, a group that defeated the required treatment plant. "We don't want the government to control us, we can handle our own problems. I run my own plant. I recognize the need to monitor my outflows. That waste is from The Valley above Malibu, all that is overdeveloped. I'm just being singled out because I'm rich."

Koolner's plant started the septic brouhaha. Twelve times over the last two years, Koolner's treatment plant has been cited by the DEP for sewage dumping violations. The plant was constructed to service the Malibu Colony condominium project, a 200-unit complex built in the hills overlooking Malibu Beach.

"You're up to something Koolner," said Slick to himself, watching the old man and his dog frighten everyone in his path.

Surfer Joe pressed his half-thumb on the button of the answering machine, and listened to the message left for Corky:

"Hey, it's Skip, I just spoke to you. You told me to give you a ring right back, so I did. I'll get back to you later, I'm going to talk to Flippy at 'Surfing World Magazine' later today. He said he was going to fill me in on Surfer Joe."

"You can't have those days, they're mine," Joe shouted at the machine. "It's you boys with your notepads and your cameras who ruined it all. You advertised the place, made your money, and moved on. Now you want to take my memories. You want to ride my past." Joe calmed down, realized he shouted over the recorded message, so, he hit the rewind button, and listened to it again.

"...Anyway, if you want to reach me, I'll be staying at Slick's place. You can find me there."

Joe clicked his cheek, adjusted his sunglasses and whispered, "Yes my kook, we will meet my kook friend."

Malibu BC (Before the Crowd.).

A fatherless fifteen-year old runaway boy stood like an unaccepted apology at Malibu. Joe sat down on the sand at The Pit, his paraffin-covered balsa board laying beside him. He wore a Navy peacoat that hung over his knees and a pair of baggy trunks. Joe warmed himself from the dawn chill with a fire made from the planks of a nearby wooden fence and a few rubber tires. He peeled and ate oranges. Joe studied the surf. Each wave was perfect. They were only three-feet. But they were absolutely perfect. The waves spiraling lines connected through all three points without sectioning. If my father was still alive, Joe thought, we'd be together. I wouldn't have run away from home. But, Joe's mother married a kook. And that's why Joe was here every day for a dawn patrol.

The teenager paddled out. The salt water rippled over his board. The ocean was glassy and gleamed with a silvery sheen—it seemed more like an potion. It was so quiet. Surfer Joe sat up and straddled his board within nature's perfect point spread. The Pacific lapped over the nose of his longboard. Kelp occasionally tugged on his dangling legs. A sea otter floated on its back and cracked open a clam on its chest. Joe smelled sage and seaweed. Tasted salt on his lips. A few feet above the water, a squadron of six pelicans cruised in a v-shaped formation. Along the shore, Joe saw sanderlings, herons, sandpipers, and further down, herons and egrets flew out of the Malibu Creek estuary. The clean water rolled underneath Joe, picking up every color and angle of light. Joe looked down. It was clear to the bottom. Fish flitted below. The reef was alive with lobsters, clams, crabs, sea urchins, and abalone.

Joe waited. A hundred feet beyond him, the hump of a wave began to form at the outside point, it was as if two fingers from an invisible giant pinched the ocean's surface like a cloth, and lifted it up, causing a crease to rise and darken. It rose until its summit became tipped with a white foam peak. Joe took off, plunged down the face, and made his a high turn for speed. The curl hooked over. Joe barely stayed ahead of the crumbling wave, riding parallel within the sling-like pocket as a curved banked escarpment rolled out before him. He ran to the nose and wrapped his ten toes on it. Joe perched and held on board's tip, which was softly embedded in the rapidly scrolling curved wall of turquoise water. This particular wave was different than any Joe had ridden, before or since. It seemed to flatten for a moment and then rise ahead of him. All he had to do was ride high for speed in the fast sections, and then just before he hit the slower sections, lean back to stall the board and allow the flatness to rise. Joe perfectly synchronized his moves with the rhythm of the wave. He maintained the same speed and pace with reform. He was so plugged into the energy of The Juice he didn't feel the wave pushing him or feel the board making any contact with the water, it was like he flying across it, levitating in a way. He was completely out of himself and connected with The Juice. It was exhilarating to get away from himself. Free from even *that*. Joe was so lost in the moment, he wondered if he was real, or if he was just something that happened as he went along. The wave just kept unfolding before him. It denied him possession but allowed him to be part of it. It offered Joe limitless possibilities. He could be whatever he wanted to be. Anything but a doctor, a lawyer, an insurance agent. Anything but one of *them*. Surfer Joe could just be himself. He didn't have to be anything. He rode it for over a thousand feet to the shore by the front of a pink house near the pier. He stepped off his board. Stood on sand. He had the place all to himself. There was nothing to stop him from coming here every day. He'd live out of anyone's car or back yard. He'd make money doing ding repairs, renting boards, or shaking change out of the pants left by kooks on the beach. He didn't have to worry about food. The ocean was an all-you-could-eat buffet. In the winter he could surf Rincon and go to the Islands. His kook stepfather wouldn't have anything to say about it. Why should Joe respect some aircraft worker from Bakersfield? A guy who didn't like surfers. They were beach bums to the stepfather. Joe's real father wasn't a beach bum to Joe. His dad was a waterman. His real father wouldn't even consider sending Joe to military school to "toughen and straighten" him up; instead, he'd teach Joe how to live off the ocean. But that wasn't good enough for Joe's stepfather because "you can't surf your life away..." Well, that might be true, Joe conceded, but how about surfing away from someone else's life?

Surfer Joe vowed to make Malibu work for him. He'd prevail over the valleys cowboys, clamdiggers, and flatlanders. The kooks were getting closer and closer to *his* Malibu. The tract housing was advancing. The kooks were establishing their positions, building their supply lines of supermarkets and freeways, passing ordinances. The kooks were coming. It was inevitable. But Joe would find some way to play the kook game without ever being part of it—no social security number, no property, no children, no bank account, no debts (well, debts he'd pay that is.). Joe would have their pleasures but never their pain. Any wave they threw at him, he'd use to his advantage. The kooks would never make him feel like a failure, the way they convinced his father to feel like a loser.

Why did this perfect world have to go away? Why must this moment fade? Joe resentfully wondered. Why? This is all he ever wanted. Why did anything have to change?

Surfer Joe paddled out and never looked back.

It was June 15, 1955.

Surfer Joe Lives

Slick studied the writing on The Wall. It was hard for Slick to accept Joe would return to Malibu, but there was one sure way to confirm Joe he was back. Slick walked to the end of the brick wall, past the metal fence, and over toward the flat area once known to Malibu locals as The Pit. In the fifties and early sixties, there was a long sandy hill everyone went down to get to the beach. Locals left their boards against the chain-link fence that ran behind it. The Pit was the best place to see the surf. But, The Pit also signified status. When Pit Crew accepted you, you were allowed to sit among them. If you weren't accepted, you definitely sat elsewhere. And if you sat elsewhere, then you better not paddle out and attempt to take their waves because you'd get run over, dropped in on, or have a board shot at your shins. Any newcomer who walked past The Pit was verbally abused by the crew:

"If you don't live here, don't surf here."

"Locals only."

"Go back to the valley."

"Kooooooooook!"

Slick was thirteen-years old. He was six feet, but skinny. The stoked boy dragged a ninety-five pound redwood-balsa board behind him, its tail partially ground down from being constantly pulled over pavement. He smiled at the Pit Crew as they reclined on their bellies in the sand and made sarcastic comments. They possessed an eminence. Slick studied the crystal waves peeling to the shore. It was so bitchin. God, he loved it here. It was the one spot where Slick didn't have to endure the taunting of any team-oriented jocks or the bullying of gear-head greasers. Here, no one cruelly ridiculed his gawky tall body, big ears, and inadequate ball-handling skills. This was his world. He was good at it.

But in 1994, The Pit was no longer a promontory point. It eroded into just a stretch of sand. Most of the rusty fence was gone too. You had to have sat there to know where The Pit once was.

"Shit, Joe is back," Slick blurted, looking down in the sand. In a huge mound, where the throne of The Pit once was, Slick stared at the definite leavings of The Malibu King.

Orange skin peels.

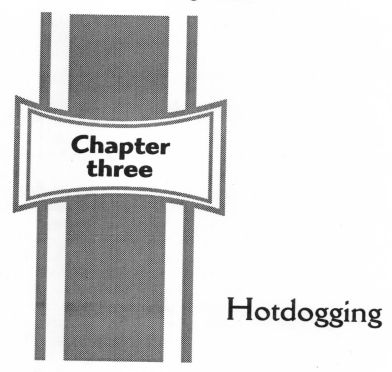

Chapter three

Hotdogging

From the Journal of Surfer Joe

The reason Toobsteak must be permanently driven out of the lineup can be found within the delicate swells of surfing's past.

Who knows how long the Polynesians surfed? Or, what century? How it began? Well, my calibrated guess is these natives were fishermen who rode waves on their boats, and then, they began trying to ride the waves in on smaller crafts. Whatever, getting back to Surfing, the Sport of Kings, or more likely, the King's Sport...the royalty, alias the Allii, ruled the Hawaiian islands through kapus, which were a tribal tradition based on royal privileges. Kapus bequeathed an entitlement of primogenitured wave peaks to the rulers, giving these elite pubahs exclusive surfing access to the best "royal" spots. The Allii were the only ones allowed to ride the highest quality boards, made from olo-trees. These boards were long, about fifteen feet, twenty-five inches wide, and seven-inches thick. The commoners rode shorter boards made of poorer wood from breadfruit trees. Boards didn't have fins back then. The natives turned by dragging their feet in the water. Surfing was taught to the natives by the Kahuna, an Hawaiian word which means teacher or great spirit. These learned watermen were versed in Ka Nalu, or the study of waves, a religion that revealed man's unity with nature through the ocean.

Then came the missionary haoles. In Hawaiian, "Ha" means "breath" and "ole" means "without." When Hawaiians held their religious ceremonies, the tribe purged their souls through deep breathing exercises. The tribe noticed the missionaries didn't breath that way in their churches, so, they were "without breath," and became known as haoles, which later became a widely used Hawaiian's disparaging term for a foreigner. Without any doubt, the haole of all haoles was Captain Cook, who along with the missionaries, discovered the happy but "misguided" pagans on Hawaii in the late 1700's. The natives at first thought Cook was the God Lono, a belief Cook encouraged, but when the natives discovered he bled like a common man and wasn't Lono, they murdered him—a good career move for Cook, but a little too late for the tribe, and Lono. The missionaries left in Cook's wake, declared surfing sinful. After all, the "misguided" natives gambled over rides, left their tasks when the surf came up, and, I bet the white holy men were really freaked by the profane sight of plainly aroused dark men coming in from their waves to juicily mount naked women in the sand. But it wasn't just the evil white haole who corrupted these allegedly innocent primitives, some of the native's own royalty were seduced by the gold and silver offered to them, and agreed to give up their ancient ways. But, I feel many of the natives were cunningly deceived instead of corrupted from within. The concept of money and owning property didn't exist in Hawaiian culture. So when they gave their land to the haole, they didn't understand how it could be his because no one owned the land, it was for everyone. The innocent Hawaiians thought the white haole a fool. So, while the missionaries told the primitives to get on their knees and look up into heavens, these holy men stole everything from the natives on earth—land, materials, culture. And surprise, by the 1900's, surfing was gone from the shores. Gone was the royalty and its kapus system. Gone was the native's family structure. Gone was the kahuna, as well as much of the Hawaiian population, which was decimated by disease. But slowly, more natives returned to their culture, some because it gave meaning to their lives, others because it enabled them to bilk more mazuma out of the tourists.

Oddly, the first man to bring surfing to the mainland was an Irish Hawaiian named George Freeth. In 1907, Freeth surfed Redondo beach as a stunt to help promote a railroad line. But the central influence was Duke Kahanamoku, an Olympic swimmer from Hawaii who demonstrated surfing throughout the world. The Duke embodied the true aloha spirit. What I particularly enjoy about the introduction of surfing to California is that the haole's religion and work ethic ruined the Hawaiian's lifestyle and destroyed surfing. Now, the Hawaiian lifestyle and surfing was coming to the mainland to ruin the misguided white man's work ethic.

Up until the fifties, only a few people searched for waves along the California coast. They drove flat-bed trucks or convertible buggies. Atop their beat-up vehicles were one-hundred-and-twenty pound redwood boards or ninety-pound hollow plywood planks. My father and Tom Blake had it all to themselves, along with Bob Simmons, Matt Kivlin, Lesley Williams, Guy Livingston, Crispy, and Joe Quigg. Eventually, the world and time drew these men away from the beach and faded into The Valley (marriage, careers, and other forms of slow-lingering death.). This left a vacuum on Malibu in the mid-fifties. Perhaps, that's what drew a drunk, and recently fired janitor, Buddy Smith, to its shores one night, where the following day, he woke up hungover in a gin-soaked suit, next to an abandoned shack in the sand. The soberly startled fat man squinted at the sun, the ocean, and the empty stretch of beach. The guy who loved eating hot dogs decided Malibu would be a good place to live in the summer. He moved into the shack and the Pit Crew grew around it. He became the grand emperor. Toob put me in charge of cleaning the kooks out of the water, while he settled disputes among valleys and the locals. The kids respected anyone who was an adult and choose not to work. It should have stayed that way, but then one day, a cute teenage girl with decent hooters, jiggled down to the beach. She dragged a longboard. We verbally abused her. She cried. Toob called us off. He became her guardian and allowed her into The Pit Crew.

That's why Toobsteak is getting taken out next.
Her.

Two women appreciatively viewed Corky's hanging corpse like an abstract modern art piece. The old man was dangling from a cord fashioned from celluloid film. His body turned clockwise then counterclockwise. A record on the stereo played the "The Gidget Does Malibu" theme song sung by the Four Sophomores:

> She's The Gidget
> My pretty little surfer girl
> She's The Gidget
> Shooting the Malibu curl

"Turn that shit off, Phrancky," commanded Annette to her cohort.

"Like, I'm not your slave," said Phrancky, rolling her eyes.

"Don't mock me," quickly said Annette.

"I didn't say anything except *no*," said Phrancky ticking her tongue off the back of her front teeth.

The two women were quite a contrast. Annette looked like an estrogen-cranked Teamster. She was in her late twenties, bulky, muscular, flat chested. She had short black hair that resembled a protective helmet of shellac. She wore bluejeans, a "Drink till she's cute" tee shirt, and workboots. In contrast, Phrancky had long blonde hair, an excellent figure she showed off in tight jeans, along with mound-bulging cleavage in a white halter top. She wore spiked red heels.

"Oooh, this is so rad, I just have to cut if off," squealed Phrancky, slashing through the film.

Corky's body thumped to the floor. The women laughed.

"We should like totally leave him," said Phrancky.

"Can't do it, no one is suppose to find a thing."

"Like, I'm not burying him—"

Annette punched her partner, knocking the attractive woman down to the floor.

"Hey, what's this macho shit?" snarled Phrancky, rubbing her face.

"I have difficulty verbalizing my thoughts," answered Annette, shrugging. "Cause you know Phrancky, you're—"

Phrancky tried to kick her. Annette saw it coming. She grabbed Phrancky's leg. Annette countered by yanking her pudgy partner down, and delivering a sharp jab to Phrancky's head.

"You dumb bitch!"

"Slut."

The stereo kept playing...

> Just grab a girl
> Have fun in the sun
> You know what to do
> With your girl at the beach in Malibu.

The two angry and aroused women thrashed on the floor, punching and scratching.

The surf magazine publisher held a clear paperweight that contained the missing half of Surfer Joe's thumb.

"Surfer Joe seems like a puzzle, but when you know all the pieces, he fits together like everyone else," said Flippy Weaver, sitting behind his desk, mulling over the eight-ounce, cup-shaped paperweight, as if he were appraising a rare stone. "You know, in the light you can still see some dirt in the nail."

"Is that really Joe's thumb?" incredulously asked Purpus.

"Yeah," said Flippy. "I found the thumb in the wreckage after the explosion at Grubby's. Thought I'd just plop it in a Dixie cup of resin." He shrugged. "Joe didn't have any use for it. Actually, it's probably the only practical thing Joe has ever done with his life."

Flippy had lost his surfer texture to time. He was in his mid fifties, short, and on the dumpy side, with a puffy layer of booze fat. He looked like a claims adjuster more than a surf publisher. He wore a gray suit, blue shirt, and red tie with a surfboard clasp. Flippy was bald, but had thick gray-streaked black hair growing on the sides of his head—it looked like a furry horseshoe thrown against his skull. Sun exposure prematurely made his skin droop around his eyes, resembling wax that hardened after melting on his face.

The "Surfing World" office was carpeted. A glass wall looked out on a working area of disheveled and underpaid people. They leaned over computer terminals within cubicles. On the walls of Flippy's office were photographs of shortboarders ripping waves apart—riding deep in a tube of water, going vertical up the face, flying through the air off a pitching lip. But, positioned below each shortboarder color picture, almost as if in a counterpoint, were Leroy Grannis old black-and-white photographs of surfers riding longboards at Dana Point, Rincon, Malibu, Swami's, and Old Man's.

"So who is Surfer Joe?" asked Purpus with a notepad in his lap, sitting in a chair across from the publisher.

Flippy leaned back in his black cushioned chair behind a mahogany desk. A computer screen was on a metal stand to Flippy's right. He put the thumb down on the surf product ads that covered his desk. "Everything Joe does is a scam. A giant scam to stay ahead of everyone. You want to see what kind of a hero he is? Ask your buddy Slick, he'll tell you what Joe is about," snorted Flippy. "Joe's just a glorified con man. A hustler. And I'll tell you something, for all his anti-surfing establishment talk, he couldn't handle it when he was no longer the top guy, and the new names came in. That's the truth of him." He yawned. "Actually, I don't care. When you get through Joe's legend and myth stuff, Joe's just a real jerk."

"So, you don't *really* have a strong opinion of the guy," said Purpus, smirking.

"Look, I hate to burst your bubble, but that beach bum image of Malibu is something the surf industry has been using for years to sell shit," said Flippy. "That real hard-core Pit Crew were like gypsies, really. They'd take anyone for anything. They were misfits, social rejects. Malibu was the *only* place where they'd get the most out the scene with the least amount of effort. Why do you think they called them surfers? And you mean to tell me you don't think those guys had egos? Come on! They were all highly competitive. They dominated Malibu. They had taken their surfing world as far as it could go, and they wanted more recognition." He paused. "They wanted the money. And that's what Sally Koolner did for everyone. She brought all that together. And all of us had a name to make good money off and never looked back. Except Joe, he wanted to be a star, like James Dean. He really tried to go Hollywood. Joe wanted to parlay his anti-kook character as the new antihero. He tried to make the spin work the other way for his career, by attacking what happened to Malibu. That guy made himself an image: the 'soul surfer' who wouldn't bow to all the commercialism, right? So, How come he was a surf stunt double in any beach movie that came down the pike? He surfed in 'The Gidget' too!" Flipped opened his desk drawer and took out a long stick of beef jerky. He bit off a chunk and chewed as the spoke. "Surfer Joe walked around like a monk, pontificating about refusing to sell his soul to promote the surf industry. The whole thing was a persona hype to promote himself. How come he charged people to use his photos in magazines? Some rebel. How come he sold his own signature board? Sold his own tee shirt? Even stickers!" Flippy paused. "Joe says he hates surf magazines, but he has a thousand bucks of my money to write a piece that he'll probably never give me." He yawned, showing gold-bridge work. "I don't care."

"So you—"

"Does anyone ask me about point stylists like Simmons, Dale Velzy, Mike Doyle, Pete Peterson, Lance Carson, Phil Edwards, Johnny Fain, Tommy Zahn, Mickey Dora, Dave Rochlen, Mickey Munoz, Vicki Flaxman, Dave Sweet, Johnny Rice, Kemp and Denny Aaberg, Kit Horn, Peter Cole, Buzzy Trent, Chubby Mitchell, Tom Morey, Hap Jacobs? Or even ask me about other surfs spots. Or other offbeat guys like Mike Eaton? No, it's always Malibu and Surfer Joe. Fuck it. How come everyone else ruined Joe's Malibu? Well, fuck him. I don't care, really. He ruined his Malibu, not just the magazines." Flippy tore off another chunk of jerky. "Joe tried to turn everything in a game. I think he did it to keep people away. He loves games. He'd come over to my place to play darts or ping pong, but it'd always be for money. And he'd make up the rules as the game would go along and always win somehow. You know, he thought he was taking kooks the whole time, but I don't think it ever dawned on him that sometimes people knew what he was up to but let him pull a scam off because they felt sorry for him."

"Why feel sorry for him?"

"Joe worshiped his dad," said Flippy. "Joe's dad taught him surfing, shaped his board. His dad blew his brains out. Joe never accepted it was a suicide. He felt the kooks' world and values killed his dad, or, made his dad feel like a failure. Joe's always been angry. His mother, who was a real nice lady, who surfed real well, remarried. I think she did it to provide for Joe. The stepfather and Joe didn't get along. He sent him to military school. Joe never forgave her. He's big on never forgiving anybody. But it's his dad death that shaped Joe. It wasn't what happened to Malibu. I could care less either way. I never had much use for the guy."

"But Joe did have the whole place to himself," said Purpus.

"Slick is the real story, he's the true prince of the point. The shortboard killed Slick. Ruined him. It was in 1966 at San Diego..."

The San Diego contest made a long story short.

Slick blandly looked at the cover of his new November "Surfing World" issue of 1966. Slick was suppose to be on the cover. The magazine was working up an entire piece all about him. But this one contest in San Diego changed everything. Instead of "Johnny Slickmeyer Longboard Champion," there was Matt carving the face of the wave. In huge letters on the cover: "Shortboard revolution begins!" Slick sucked in his lips, shook his head, and opened the issue to read the article that was his epitaph, as well as the tombstone for the longboard era:

Matt Young takes World Surfing
Championship in San Diego

Noseriding is dead.

The United States Surfing Federation team was blown off the waves by Australian Matt "The Animal" Young.

The contests clearly showed the new wave of surfing is going to be ridden on smaller boards. Matt tore the waves apart with sharp and snappy cutbacks off the lips, and floaters. He connected through every section. He buried his rails so deep on turns he was nearly vertical to the water.

"No longer does surfing have to be defined by just going in a straight line across the wave," said Young. "In the old days surfers rode straight into shore. Another longboard appeared that it made it possible for others to go straight across the wave. My shorter board makes it possible for the board to go up and down the wave. I can make more moves closer to the curl. I can make blunt directional changes. I don't do what the wave tells me to do. I attack it. "

Matt ripped on a nine-and-half foot board with a curved "hydrodynamic" fin. But what set the board apart was its Bob McTavish vee bottom also designed by George Greenough. The vee-shape is a ridge in the middle of the tail of the board, actually its more of a crease, and the tail's bottom is slanted upwards from the ridge to the rails, which enables the board to drive and accelerate better on turns.

"I was doing two turns to Slick's one. Slick's in the Dark

Ages. He was surfing in like Phil Edwards or Lance Carson," said Matt.

Slick took exception to Young's radical viewpoint.

"I like Phil Edwards and Lance Carson, they have style, I'll take that as a compliment," responded Slick. "Watching those two is like a flowing dance. Every step, every maneuver, had a function, and they used subtle shifts of weight. There was something regal about them. And they made it all look easy. I surf *with* the wave not against it. I got a nine-second noseride in the finals and it meant nothing."

Slick was at the peak of his career wave. Without any warning, his original style became prehistoric, his board an antique, and his future non-existent. The shortboard stuffed him into the world of the unmakeable forever. Shortboards. Slick couldn't even stand on the things. They skidded out from under his feet. These shortboarders didn't want longboarders in their ocean. Kids that were thirteen-years old jeered Slick's graceful cutbacks, shoulder leads, and nose rides. Why? Because he wasn't "doing" anything on the waves. They swore at Slick if his longer board caught the wave before them, called him an "old man," and dismissed his board as a "tanker." Many longboarders didn't want to fight over waves with someone half their age, they paddled to shore and put their energies into families and careers. Slick had no desire to lose a distinctive style he spent his life perfecting. He didn't leave. The ocean was the only thing he loved, the only thing he had. He kept paddling out.

But...it was over.

From the Journal of Surfer Joe

I fully realize my journal will fall into kook hands, and since most of you kooks don't surf, you don't know the difference between the design of a longboard and a shortboard. Longboarding is pure poetry. Shortboarding is chaotic, aggressive, and looks more like skateboarding than surfing to me—they turn a wave into a wall.

Here's how I have to break it down for your limited minds...

The Traditional Longboard

Length: nine feet and above.

Weight: Between twenty-five to thirty-five pounds.

Nose: Round. Eighteen inches (measured twelve inches from the tip.).

Tail: Square tail. Fourteen to fifteen inches (measured twelve inches from the bottom).

Width: Twenty-three to twenty-five inches. (measured across widest part of the board.)

Thickness: Three to three-and-a-half inches.

Basic Longboard Design: The length restricts the rider to long drawn turns. The sides of the board (known as rails) are rounded and soft, which allows water to wrap around the board, giving the surfer more control. Soft rails also make the board more forgiving, allowing it to adjust by sliding up and down the wave or to plow through bumpy sections of water. These boards have very little rocker (which is the curvature in the tail to the nose of the board). However, less rocker makes it more difficult for the rider to take off on steeper waves without burying the nose of the board, which is called purling. But because the bottoms are flat, it's easier to glide, paddle, and gives them more planing speed. The board has a single fin that is usually nine inches or longer.

There are three ways to ride a traditional longboard: one, your weight must be over the tail to turn it; two, you have to move to the middle of the board to gain speed; and three, you can stand on the nose to slow the board down; or, depending on the design of the board, accelerate.

The Typical Shortboard

Length: Around six feet to six feet four-inches

Weight: Eight to twelve pounds.

Nose: Semi-pointed or very pointed.

Tail: Squash tail, which is a rounded tail with hard edges, sometimes they have with a wing (a little rail line extension used as a pivot point). Thirteen or thirteen inches wide.

Width: Around nineteen inches.

Thickness: Two and a half inches.

Basic shortboard design: The typical shortboard has a tear-drop shape (the tip of the tear is the nose). Most shortboards have a major curved bottom, and a lot of kick in the nose and tail, giving them a potato chip look. The pronounced rocker makes them more maneuverable. The nose is pointed for better wave entry making it easier for the rider to take off in steeper waves without burying the nose of the board. The shortboard's rails are hard edged, almost like the corner of a table. These harder rails skim over the surface of a wave's face, and break loose easily for snappy quick turns. The bottom of the board has vee in the tail, which enables the board to drive and accelerate on turns. Less water resistance translates into more speed and quicker turns. It's as if water is the *enemy* of the shortboard. The board has a five-and-half inch center fin, with two smaller side fins, one on each side. These fins give the board a tighter turning radius.

There is only one way to ride shortboards: butt-wiggling. A shortboarder turns and generates power from staying in one spot and pumping the board from the tail. Shortboarders thrive in fast hollow waves and tube rides. They live to move vertically up the face, smack their board off the top and float down into the shoulder, or hit the pitching lip and pull an aerial, which is successfully executed by having the wave launch the board into the air, and drop back into the wave.

Conclusion

Shortboarding is for a young body. They can't last. They're the stuff of chiropractor's dreams. You're older for a longer time than you're young, so, develop a style that goes the distance.

There you have it.

"Slick just couldn't adapt to the transition," said Flippy, picking the jerky from his teeth with plastic surfboard-shaped letter opener. "In just a few years after 1966, the average length of a board went from ten feet to six feet. No one wanted a longboard, anymore. No one cared about it. Slick's signature longboard was dead. Man, classic longboards were stripped of their glass and sawed in half to make shortboards. No one hung out in surf shops. They were closed everywhere. The shops were replaced by stoned-out, back-yard shapers who air brushed psychedelic peace signs on their boards. They talked about their "being" and 'soul,' but surfed viciously and competitively for each wave in the water."

"Do you think Surfer Joe found the perfect wave?" asked Purpus.

"If Joe did, he wouldn't tell you where it was," authoritatively said Flippy. "And if Joe didn't, he'd try to give you the impression he knew where it was. Either way, Joe'd be real convincing."

Deep behind enemy lines in The Valley...

Surfer Joe was rattled. He had just been released from prison for credit-card fraud. A guest of the government for three years. Now, Joe was stuck in a court-ordered job. In a month, he'd be finished to the satisfaction of the federales. He wanted out of this country. He was thirty-seven years old. He leaned against his stepfather's car in the driveway. He didn't want to be there. This house was one of many homes in an area built for defense workers. Typical adobe style. Stucco sides that looked like cheap icing on a day-old cake. A terra-cotta red tiled roof. Minuscule front yard and a smaller back yard. Each house nearly pressed against the one beside it.

"The surf star," sarcastically said Joe's stepfather, emerging from the house's front door. He was seventy-two, bald, big chested with a slightly puffed out stomach. "Is that what they call ex-cons these days? Surf stars?"

"I came to get my stick," said Joe, pointing to a ten-foot balsa board laying on the neatly trimmed green lawn.

"Some surf legend," said the old man, sitting down on the steps "Do all surf legends get arrested? Do all surf legends have strangers call their parents' home demanding money their son stole from them? Or, threaten to sue because their son hit them in the head with his surfboard? You broke your mother's heart. It's a good thing she didn't live to see this day."

"If she was alive she'd probably wonder why she married a kook like you," said Joe.

"Kook, you say that a lot don't you? What is a kook? You're always calling people kooks."

"Kook, it's from the Hawaiians. They spelt it 'k-u-k," said Joe in a professorial tone. "It's the Hawaiian word for excrement."

"Yeah, that's right surf star, what does a kook like me know?" softly said the old man. "I'm such a kook I've been alive seventy years and never got arrested for anything. That's what a kook I am. Who paid the bills of all those people the surf star stiffed? But what do I know? I'm a kook. Kooks don't have feeling. Kooks don't love their mothers...their wives." He paused. "Kooks don't get   lonely." His cataracts flared. "Your mother and me! In my day—"

"Hey, I'm here to sell my board to someone," slowly said Joe. "Then, after I get my cake, I'll kick out, *dad.*" Joe fixed his gaze on the cracks in the driveway until he heard the front door close. "Go back in your mausoleum," grunted Joe to himself.

An electronic horn beeped out the opening notes for a surf song by the Surfaris called "Wipe Out." A 1951 Ford Woody parked in front of Joe's house. The car was in mint condition and had surf stickers on its side windows. The driver was a pure full-on kook in his mid-thirties. He obviously had bucks. There was an awed look in his eyes. Joe had seen these kooks before, they use to follow him around at Malibu, one even watched him change. These kooks couldn't surf so tried to achieve recognition by becoming collectors of rare surf-related items.

"Hi, Joe," said the kook.

"There's the stick," said Joe, nodding toward the grass.

"Oh man!" exclaimed the guy, picking up the old balsa board. "This is cherry! A Simmons. It's a—"

Joe wrenched out the words, "It belonged to my father." He sucked in his lower lip and looked down at the driveway. "Best board I've ever ridden." His eyes bulged into a glare. "Like, where's the bread?"

The kook pulled a wad of money from his pocket. Joe reached out for the roll. The kook pulled the cash back. Joe looked up at the man, puzzled.

"You don't remember me, do you? " vindictively asked the kook with a snotty edge in his voice. "From Malibu?"

"Uh, it's not that I don't remember you, I didn't notice you," stiffly said Joe, twitching his head to the left.

"I was around sixteen. It was my first day at Malibu. You called me a kook, then you intentionally ran me over. Sent me to the hospital. Your skeg to put a gash in my new board. Someone had to drive me to the hospital because one of your Pit Crew buddies slashed my car's tires."

"Sorry about the board."

"How do you like it playing by my rules in the real world?" asked the kook, waving the money in front of Joe's face.

"Aaaaah, like, I wouldn't know. The real world? I, uh, don't surf there, man," said Joe, clicking his cheek,

"Oh, now, did I say I was going to give you fifteen hundred dollars?" bitchily asked the kook, removing two hundreds from the roll. "Well, all I have is thirteen hundred dollars."

Joe just stood there. He needed the money. And he was still on probation so he couldn't hit the guy.

"You want to clean my clock don't you?" mockingly asked the kook, leaning toward Joe, their noses a quarter inch apart. "But you can't. You're on parole. You can't do shit to me. How does it feel now? *Kook.*"

Joe gulped in rage, stiffened and said, "Uh, if you're so superior to me, what do you have that anyone would give you thirteen hundred dollars for?" Joe snapped. "Besides a kidney."

The kook took the board, handed Joe the money, and slid the stick into the open rear window of the Woody. He drove away and shouted, "Asshole!"

Surfer Joe looked down at the money. He shook his head, ashamed. He felt like he collaborated with the enemy. The Simmons board was the only possession of his father's Joe had left. He walked from his childhood home. No one called him back for lunch.

Purpus sat alone at the table in a conference room at "Surfing World." He filtered through three folders that were thick with photographs and clippings on Surfer Joe and The Malibu Pit Crew. Strewn across the long table were numerous black-and-white glossies, a mound of news clips, and several open magazines. Purpus excitedly jotted notes down on a pad. His legs rapidly shook up and down, poised on the balls of his feet. His heart was quickly thumping. He reverently thumbed through photograph after photograph of the pre-Gidget Malibu days...surfers in bathing suits lounging in the sand along The Pit, their boards leaning on the rusty wire fence behind them...shirtless guys who were playing guitars on the beach to attractive women...Toobsteak drinking gin and sitting in an inner-tube supported couch that floated in the ocean...surfers in riding waves and no one in the water in front or behind them. Oh to have been in that Malibu, thought Purpus, no wonder those guys were unfit for anything else.

"What's this?" asked Purpus to himself, looking with surprise at an old photograph of Slick. He was skinny and still in his teens...

Slick and an ten-year old boy paddled on longboards in the Atlantic ocean. There was a crowd of about twenty people floating in the water. But these two were the farthest ones out. It was only a three-foot day, but the waves looked enormous to the boy. It seemed like they were miles away from the Jersey shore. Purpus was pumped up. Slick was going to teach him how to surf. The boy was always in awe of this older California cousin. Slick was so cool. A surf star on tour to promote his signature longboards. The dark native-like tan. The deep blue eyes. The sun-bleached blonde hair. He was lean. No fat. All defined muscle. He seemed invincible. So confident. And women were crazy about him! They sent Slick naked pictures of themselves. Slick even showed them to him. Man, did Purpus want to be a surfer.

"My grandmother paddles better than that," said Slick, straddling his board on the undulating ocean.

"I'm trying," groaned the boy, weakly slapping the water, his hands seemed to slide off the surface instead of penetrate it.

A wave rose.

"Turn around, Skip, and face the beach," said Slick, pointing to the shore. "This one is all yours, go for it. Paddle hard now! Angle your board, man. Go!"

The boy paddled. The flat surface in front of him sucked up and rose underneath the board. He stared down into what looked like a twenty-foot gorge. He wanted to back out. It was too far a drop. He stopped. But, the board went forward. Slick shoved its tail! The boy went down the wave as it curled and rose behind him.

"Noooo," he screamed.

Purpus clung to the board. It was moving by itself. He tried to stand up. The pitching curl of the wave knocked him into the water. As the boy fell, he looked to his right and saw his riderless board angled in perfect trim across the green shoulder. The closing lip drove the boy down to the bottom. It knocked all the air out of him. He spun around and around in greenness and bubbles. Where was Slick? thought the boy, doesn't he know I'm going to drown?

After what seemed like several minutes, the wave's turbulence released him. Purpus rapidly clawed to the surface. He burst through the water, breathing deeply, sounding like a broken vacuum cleaner. The boy's nostrils hacked salt water. His lungs ached.

"Your mouth full of sand crabs?" said Slick, laughing.

"Help," shouted the boy, his eyes panicky.

"You want to surf, learn to hold onto your stick," said Slick, who had retrieved the boy's board, and shoved it toward him. "My cousin's a hodad."

Purpus gratefully grasped the board.

"Here comes one," said Slick, paddling in front of the moving and rising bulge. He powerfully stroked through the water, hardly making a splash. Slick smoothly slid into the wave and stood and turned in a fluid motion. He seemed to daydream through the ride. The boy marveled at how Slick stayed right in the perfect spot, just ahead of the curl. Slick used the board like a wand, passing it over the water and conjuring up the wave's shape. He swung his board back into the pitching white water, swept it around to the right again, and slid into the reformed shoulder that eluded the boy. Purpus saw the rising shoulder as a place where you could learn to be free, and in command, sweeping, dropping and climbing. Styling,

As Purpus looked at the progression of Surfer Joe pictures, he noticed a development of Joe's image. In the early photographs, Surfer Joe was very gangly, but there was a playful mischeviousness in his face. There wasn't any posing, or crouching, or arches. But as Surfer Joe's audience increased, he cultivated his rebel persona with calculated poses...Joe giving judges the BA on a contest wave...Joe in beach conversation with Henry Miller...Joe in a Nazi uniform...Joe shoving people off waves or shooting his board at them...Joe flipping off the camera or shielding his face from it...Joe picking his nose.

Purpus found a magazine clipping taped to the back of a photograph. It had a picture of Grubby with an obituary tribute piece written about him:

Gidget Must Die

Surf Pioneer
Grubby Devine
(1926 - 1961)

Grubby Devine was a chemical engineer who helped create polyurethane foam. This foam enabled surfboard manufacturers to mass produce boards through the use of molded blanks. The Devine blank has been used to make surfboards since 1960. It became a multi-million dollar a year industry during the sixties surfing boom.

Unfortunately, Devine never lived to cash in on his discovery. He was killed in an acetone explosion at his surf shop. Also injured was Surfer Joe Campion.

Devine used his military experience with the development of fiberglass materials in World War Two to create polyurethane.

"Everyone was scrambling to develop a foam blank," said Francis Koolner, Devine Foam president, "Redwoods were too heavy, balsa was lighter with varnish, but they absorbed water. When polystyrene came in, people experimented with it. But Devine was the first one to put urethane in the mix, and made quality foam blanks. It's the same blank we've been selling since the fifties."

Skip remembered how Corky Barber felt uncomfortable discussing the surf shop explosion that took Grubby Devine's life. Grubby had perfected the foam blank formula, thought Skip, yet Koolner and his Malibu Pit Crew benefited from Grubby's laborious experiments, and used the foam as the foundation for The Crew's multi-million dollar surf industry. How did Koolner's crew wind up with everything? And why wasn't Joe in on the deal? After all, wasn't Joe the consummate hustler, the user of all users, the man who feared surrendering to the day job? Did Koolner eliminate Grubby to attain his own personal formula for success? After all, Devine Foam went into just about every surfboard made since 1960. This dominance of the foam blank market was achieved by Koolner's ambition. The old man had an unlimited money supply. He ruthlessly stuffed any potential competitor by undercutting their price, even at a loss to himself. Eventually, he bankrupted them. Koolner cut off foam blanks supplies to any surfboard manufacturer who even tried another blank. Skip felt that anyone who was already rich, but would still be competitively brutal to increase his fortune, had to be capable of an even harsher form of elimination to narrow down the competition. But, if Surfer Joe wasn't in on the profits, and Koolner did whack Devine, why didn't Joe implicate Koolner in Devine's death? Or, at least blackmail him? Maybe Slick would offer to fill him in the gray spots. But, if Slick didn't offer, Purpus wasn't going to press his cousin.

The remaining magazine articles in the files dealt with numerous lawsuits and court appearances by Surfer Joe. One was dated September, 5, 1967.

Surfer Joe gets wiped out in court

After losing in his day at court, Surfer Joe Campion said he will leave Malibu in a quest to find the perfect wave.

Surfer Joe, who has done everything to promote his image as the rebel surfer became a victim of his own notoriety. He filed the suit a year ago against Francis Koolner and Corky Barber film distribution for using surf footage taken of him. The suit claimed Barber used Joe's image without his permission. The court determined Joe was a public figure who lost his right to privacy.

"I mean how can he own me? It doesn't seem right. I don't even own my surfing style anymore," lamented Joe. "All those guys made money around me, I just wanted to surf. I'm not trying to make money, I'm trying to get what they made off me."

Joe has lost several suits over the years.

"It's a typical scam that has Surfer Joe all over it," said Koolner. "If he hates kooks why does he use lawyers all the time? He does it because he finds some lawyer who is willing to work on a contingency, so if he wins Joe gets money, if he loses Joe doesn't have to pay him."

"Koolner and his Pit Crew destroyed my Malibu, they can have it," said Joe. "I'm going to find a place that's better. Back to the purity of the primeval away from civilization. I'm going to find Malibu's twin sister."

"I'll tell you why he's leaving Malibu, because Joe knows I'm going to counter sue him for my court costs," said Koolner. "What Joe is really mad about is I beat him at his own game."

It was ironic, thought Skip, Surfer Joe created a rebel image as the King of Malibu to promote himself into movie roles, which it did, Surfer Joe played numerous minor parts in nearly every beach exploitation surf flick. But, Joe's notoriety elevated him into the level of a public figure, which meant he couldn't control his image as Surfer Joe. Surfer Joe, like his overrun Malibu, now belonged to the public domain of the kooks. Without even paying Joe, anyone could film him riding waves or hanging out at the beach. All Joe could do was hope to make money by building his legend to capitalize on future opportunities or cons, so Joe announced his search for the perfect wave and disappeared. The kooks wondered where Joe surfed, freelance photographers took shots of him throughout the world, and reporters paid to interview him. Sometimes Joe kept his name up by periodically selling an article to Surfing World to make a few bucks—the articles were screeds, denouncing the commercialism of surfing. Joe's very absence from the Malibu scene promoted his presence.

Purpus picked up the next clipping. It was dated 1974. He read the outcome of Joe's hustling career:

Surfer Joe sentenced on fraud charges

Joe Campion, known as Surfer Joe, received a seven-year sentence today in Los Angeles Superior Court on fraud charges.

The tanned, blonde-hair, blue-eyed surf legend, fidgeted in a suit. The thirty-five year old man stood silently as Judge Robert Mosely sentenced him.

The charges dealt with Campion's theft of several credit cards, as well as the use of other people's checks. Campion used the funds to take international trips, enjoy luxurious ski weekends, as well as exorbitant restaurant meals. In other cases, he made purchases with the credit cards and sold the items for money.

When the charges were filed in 1968, Campion never appeared in court. Instead, he left the country, and lived abroad in resorts where he worked various jobs. Campion voluntarily turned himself into Federal authorities one month ago.

With good behavior, Campion could be out in three years, according to court officials.

"Hmmm," said Skip, sucking on a cherry Lifesaver. The caged con man probably never forgave himself for not beating that section, thought Purpus.

"See what I mean?" asked Flippy, standing by the door of the room. He tossed the Surfer Joe paperweight with one hand and caught it as he spoke. "Look, Surfer Joe was just a hustler who got out of control. What seemed like a game to take the kooks became crimes. He lost focus. It started out by stealing change out of pants left by Valleys on the beach. It advanced into promising to shape a board for a guy, take the money and stiff him. Then it went into another plane. Joe'd go to parties and take furs out of closets or off beds. It wasn't enough. He started using people's checks and credit cards—then, he got busted." Flippy chuckled. "Joe's a user. Hey, we're not talking about a guy who is twenty. We're talking about a guy who is well into his fifties. Nobody wants to see *that* Surfer Joe. And what does he have? The guy really has nothing. No wife. No kid. No career. No accomplishment. All he has is his King Of Malibu legend. That's why he tries to protect it."

"You think Joe'll ever come back?"

"If he does, it's not going to be pleasant."

When Surfer Joe walked past the fat man at the counter, Joe nearly tripped on the leg of a stand displaying "Malibu Surfing Museum" t-shirts. He smoothly recovered his stride and began perusing the exhibits in the converted beach cottage.

"I'm sorry but we're closing in five minutes," courteously said Toobsteak, munching on a relish-packed hot dog as he read the personal ads in a weekly newspaper. He sat on a stool behind a counter by a cash register, which had a postcard display beside it. Outside of a few wrinkles, Joe noted Toob hadn't changed much. He was a fat in the fifties and, now, he was fat in his late sixties. He had a puffy face and red smears on his road-kill like splattered nose. His thinned hair was combed straight back, but Joe could see lines of pink flesh between each strand.

"Um, I'll only be a minute," said Joe, speaking in a low but slightly disguised voice.

Toob smiled, his eyes brightened, and with his mouth full of food he said, "Oh, hell, take your time and look around. I have nowhere to go anyway, I still have a dinner to finish." He put down the paper and added. "Nice little place, huh?"

"It's exactly what I expected," said Joe, his face concealed beneath the floppy brim of a large feather-strewn canvas hat.

The Malibu Surfing Museum predictably displayed a highly inaccurate portrayal of Malibu, thought Joe, which made sense, largely because the museum was supported and donated by Koolner, not through any philanthropic impulse, but because zoning laws wouldn't allow him to develop the cottage into a condo, and he needed a tax shelter. Every exhibit reinvented the history of Malibu to promote Koolner's surf industry products as "classics," mainly because they were derived from a long traditional of surfing's past.

Joe stood before various pictures devoted to the manufacture of surfboards, which displayed Devine Foam.

"Devine Foam made so much money, I wouldn't have the time to spend all the money they made," jovially said Toob. "And, see that picture of Kahuna shaping longboards under the pier? He's still shaping. He's working on some new modern longboard." Toob unwrapped another hot dog. "Kahuna made a lot of money patenting his leash cord. Some people hated the leash, but I figure it just brings more people in the water, they want to enjoy the same thing everyone else does: surf and sun."

"Huh, I thought Kahuna was dead," said Joe, browsing.

There was a glass case containing surfboard manufacturers decals, Iron Crosses, early issues of "Surfing World" magazine, original Murphy cartoons, unopened Dick Dale and Beach Boys albums, along with a Ed "Big Daddy" Roth Surf Fink model. These items meant nothing to Joe. It was all kook paraphernalia—things kooks purchased so people around them would know they were surfers.

Joe stood before an entire wall devoted to *her* and *that* movie. He stared at stills from the flick, showing actors who were much better looking than their real-life counterparts, as well as scenes where the surfing actors allegedly rode waves, their hair perfectly combed, and dry. There was even a shot of Joe surfing. He hung his head.

"You know, I was one of the original Pit Crew, we were the only ones on the beach back then," said the fat man, getting up from his chair and walking over to Joe. "I built the shack. I'm Toobsteak!" He was surprised the man didn't even react. "They called me Toobsteak because all I ate was hot dogs. I use to stick my arms straight out to my side and do the Iron Cross and just go right into shore." He stuck out his arms. "Like this. The man didn't even turn around. "We had a reunion a couple years ago. I didn't recognize anybody. I think it was because I was so drunk back then I don't remember anyone."

Toob laughed, expecting the man to smile, ask a question; or, at least be impressed with his legendary status.

"Do you keep the boards back there?" asked Joe, walking toward a back room.

"Yeah, we're just storing them for now because we want to set up a display," said Toob, following the man.

The men stood amid two dozen old longboards in the dimly lit back room. The vertical vintage sticks leaned sideways in their slots. Some were hollowed-out paddleboards, others were solid redwood or balsa.

"Yep, these boards are works of art," said Toobsteak, taking a bite of his hot dog and spewing fragments.

"Surfing is a work of art, the board is just a stage," sharply corrected Surfer Joe, pulling out his left arm to pick up the balsa longboard from the rack.

Toobsteak saw the slight stump on the man's left hand.

"Joe," Toob blurted, a piece of a hot dog dropping from his mouth to the floor.

"Yes, my friend,""said Joe, glaring, wheeling around with the board.

Toobsteak ran down the aisle. Joe pursued him. The heaving fat man tripped over the leg of the t-shirt stand. He landed flat on his back. Toob looked up. He saw the bottom of a surfboard descending upon him. It crushed down on his chest, pinning his arms. Toob squirmed. Surfer Joe's eyes peered down over the board's nose.

"Time to get happy, Steak," sprightly said Joe, showing his gap-toothed smile. "Let's go surfing."

Koolner sat at the sixteenth century desk and stared at his masterpiece. The old man sipped a Margaux that was older than him. If Joe kept eliminating Koolner's potential opposition, the old man reasoned, there was nothing to really stop Koolner from achieving his ultimate Malibu coup. He looked through the huge glass windows at the human specks riding the moonlit waves.

Koolner envisioned how glorious it would be not to see any waves and all the surfers standing on the beach looking at nothing. That day would come, he thought, that day will definitely come. Only Surfer Joe could stop him, and maybe Slick, but Koolner doubted that. Surfers didn't have the time to acquire money or political clout, they were too busy surfing. No surfer could achieve my lifestyle, gloatingly concluded Koolner, proudly surveying his abode. The marble flooring covered with woven rugs. Cathedral ceiling. Track lighting. A wine cellar. Expensive Southwestern modern art on the wall. Glass tables with driftwood sculptures. One corner of the room contained a towering stereo system and a large TV screen, and on either side of this entertainment center were shelves filled with hundreds of laser discs. On the opposite wall, were numerous Chamber of Commerce awards, citations, and civic plaques, and several pictures of Koolner surrounded by businessmen holding silver shovels at groundbreaking ceremonies. The outside wall was made of tinted glass and had the best and highest ocean view of The Malibu. A widow's walk ran outside the place (It also had a five-person jacuzzi.). Koolner, smacked the wine with his tongue, rolling its silky texture around his mouth. The old man folded his Malibu masterplan. A letter fell from the document. The Gidget received it three months ago from Joe:

> *I've found the perfect wave. I've found the perfect place. I'm coming back to get you. And we'll be free.*
> Love
> Surfer Joe

Joe could easily be handled, thought Koolner, he's a psycho. The phone rang. Koolner picked it up but said nothing.

"Joe's in Toob's shack," said the voice at the other end.

Koolner, hung up. He put the letter down, unrolled the sheets to his engineering masterpiece, and poured himself another glass of wine. He looked over the rim of his glass and out to the human specks on the ocean. They reminded Koolner of the flies on the surface of unprocessed sludge in a tank at his sewage treatment plant.

"Goodbye surfers," said the old man, toasting his glass high. "Goodbye Malibu."

"Toob, you're about to become a *true* tubesteak," said Surfer Joe, attaching the last of the gasoline cans from the ceiling. "A surf sacrifice of the ultimate hotdogger." He tilted his head. "How do you like your new beach shack?"

Toobsteak stood underneath a tepee-like shelter of five longboards. He was tied against one of the museum's support beams. Toob was completely enclosed in a red body bag. There was an air hole by his mouth. The bag was filled with black powder comprised of sulfur, saltpeter, and charcoal.

"Why do this to me?" bleated Toobsteak, trying to peak through the bag's opening.

"When you explode, Steak, the compression hitting the gas cans will shoot the place up into a ball of flames," calmly said Joe, climbing down the ladder. "Double-base propellants. Some great brisance." Joe clicked his cheek, examining his work. "It's amazing what you can learn if you don't go to college."

"I took care of you, Joe," warbled Toobsteak.

"Yes, uh, I remember how you lent a hand on my behalf,'"said Joe, holding up his stump.

"When you were a little gremmie you were a crybaby," said Toob. "Someone always had to swim in and get your board for you. And I did that. I gave you rides. I was good to you Joe. You wanted to be taken care of and I took care of you."

Joe looked down. He seemed ashamed.

"I was like a father to you—"

"You weren't my father!" screamed Joe, completely enraged. "If you were a father you wouldn't desert me. You should have protected me. I just wanted to surf. That's all I wanted."

"I'm not one of them Joe, you know I'm not," blubbered Toobsteak. "After what happened to you and Grubby, I never took nothing from them. All I ever wanted to do was just live in that beach shack. I never sold out my Malibu days."

Joe's anger subsided, taking with it any form of remorse. He ignored Toob's pleas. Joe happily continued to sprinkle gray flash powder on the twenty-foot fuse that stretched from the giant human hot dog to the door.

"Joe!" begged Toob.

"Joe?" asked Surfer Joe, lighting a match. "Joe? I don't see any Joe. Don't worry, Steak, this isn't *me* doing this." He tapped his sunglasses. "You know, you and this museum will have a lot in common, in a few seconds, you'll both become history."

"Joe, they would have killed you if I wasn't there, please—"

"My job was to keep the kooks out of the water," petulantly said Joe, bending down to the fuse with the burning match. "Your job as President of The Pit was to police the land, keep the kooks out. But, then you allowed that tattle-tailing bitch down to the beach!" It took a brief moment for Joe's point to connect with Toob's mental wave.

"You're doing this to me because of The Gidget!" Toob sniffled, jarred.

"Gidg...Gidg...Gidg..." sputtered Joe.

Joe was transported back into The Black Tube. The voices soothingly chanted within the watery circular walls, "Gidget must die, Gidget must die, Gidget must die." Joe was calm and relaxed. He didn't hear the approach of the dark surfer behind him. Ahead, through the swirling opening he saw an orb of flaming brightness. Joe effortlessly shot out of the Black Tube into the light. The wave compressed and collapsed behind him, spitting out a spray of heat on his shoulders.

"Styling," said Joe, arching his back with his hands at his sides, toes bending his sandals over the edge of the curb as if he were hanging ten.

Behind Joe, was the flaming closeout of the Pit Crew's past. Surfer Joe clicked his cheek. "Made that section."

From the Journal Of Surfer Joe

Everyone has a home break. A secret spot that serves no purpose, no career advancement or security. But it's the one place we're the happiest. It's the place we see more of ourselves than anywhere else. It's our true pitch. But it's never safe there. Times will change and someone will destroy it, try to make money from it. We reason, why not get in on the ground floor? Make the money. It's all going to happen, anyway. So we corrupt our secret spot. But once we depart, we're less of ourselves forever, and part of the world even more. My home break was Malibu. There's a Malibu in everyone. Everyone rides it once. But to have it and actually *be* in Malibu. It's a wave no one would ever want to get off. My summer was my Malibu. My Malibu summer became everyone's summer. My summer was dead.

I will die within it.

So will you.

Chapter four

Coming up

"Like tomorrow it'll be tits," said the tan young bartender. He had dyed blonde hair. He wore a baseball cap backwards. The kid was dressed in a neon shirt and pants. He pushed a beer in front of a sullen Slickmeyer. "I'm squirting you this brew, you're buffed." He paused. "How was the surf? Tubular, brah?"

"Well, braaaaah, there were too many people, braaaaah," sarcastically said Slick, sitting at the bar of the Malibu Boardriders Club.

"Hellah surf, it'll be really perf mañana. Gnarly waves, brah. Going to be mondo crowds," said the bartender, pointing out the window, which gave a view of The Bu from the end of the pier. The refracted ocean lines of waves were illuminated by the full moon. "Can you believe it? There are forty guys out there surfing!"

Slick looked out into the darkness. He saw shadowy figures. They wore fluorescent lime-green armbands. They streaked across the water. He sipped his beer.

"I bet they're tuning up for that bogus Malibu contest this weekend," said the bartender. "Total buttheadage, brah. But it'll be cool to scope the beach for choice nuggets. Big Mac a few." A girl in a black halter top and tight Spandex pants walked by. The kid and Slick turned to watch her. The kid slapped his hand flat on the bar, and growled, "Smack it!" He did some inner-city dance step done from some rap group. Slick laughed. He liked the kid.

"Did you see this, brah?" asked the bartender, pushing a red piece of paper across the bar to Slick. "It's pretty rad. Someone's been putting them up on phone poles."

The flyer stated:

Protest Malibu's Professional
Surfing Contests

The surf contests held on beaches don't have the legal right to keep you from surfing the ocean. Their contest permit only entitles them to the use of the beach.

This Saturday for "The Gidget Longboard Invitation" paddle out in the water and surf.

If anyone lays a hand on you, you can sue or have them arrested for assault!

"This must be what Koolner was bitching about," said Slick, laughing. "Good, I hope everyone shows up. Let them all fight it out." Slick scowled and looked around the joint. "God, does this place suck, or what?"

Kooks loved the Malibu Boardriders Club, but Slick despised it's mega-kooked-out touristy feel. The walls were wicker paneled and adorned with fishnets festooned from fake bamboo pole supports. Throughout the place hung framed pictures depicting Leroy Grannis' classic black-and-white images of surfers in the pre-Gidget days. Kooks came for the atmosphere. But Slick went because the draft beer was cheap.

A Beach Boys song called "Do it Again" started playing on the bar's jukebox:

It's automatic and dark with gold fins
And the conversation turns to girls we knew
When their hair was soft and long
And the beach was the place to go
Sun tan bodies and waves of sunshine
California girls and a beautiful coastline
Get together
And do it again

"Stokaboka!" yelled a fat guy wearing a 'Gidget Longboard Invitational' cap. The fat guy was one of many middle-aged men near the juke box. They hooted and drunkenly danced. They all wore the identical surf club insignia tee shirts, jeans, and sandals.

"Stokaboka," repeated Joe in disgust. His face twisted.

"Brah, why so chapped? If you like think this place is so hiddy, why are you here?"

"Meeting a bro, *brah*,"

"Cowabunga!" yelled another fat guy, spilling his beer as he did a surfing gesture.

"Surfer's stomp!" shouted his friend, shuffling his feet and then bouncing on one foot.

"Look at'em," said Slick, his eyes grimly fastened upon the surf club members. He took a pull on his beer. "Surf wannabes that never were. They were kooks then and they're kooks now. They want everyone to think they're surfers, because in the water, they don't know *how* to surf. In the sixties they were pseudos with peroxide hair, Pendleton shirts, and jams, playing guitar or bongos. Now they're all coming back to surfing. Trying to buy back what they missed with their Gold cards. Well, I don't have to relive it. I've been living it." He glared harder at the group. "Those assholes will bring the worst of surfing back with them too. You watch what they bring into longboarding: sponsorships, surf clubs, team riders, rigged contests, photo shoots, and surf videos. And what will you have? The same phony image again in magazines. A whole bunch of wing nuts surfing *proficiently* with other surfer's postures, hanging ten toes on the nose, looking casual, perfect—and soulless."

"Brah, you're so live!" said the bartender, laughing. "You know, there was an old dude just in here who was saying the same rap."

"What did he look like?" said Slick, surprised. He held the beer to his lips.

"Blonde hair, tan, about your age range, you know, an old fart," said the bartender, making a cocky smile.

"Was he missing part of his thumb?"

"He was *missing* something, brah. The dude was seriously spinned. He was playing with his shades, kinda hunched over. Real hincky. He hated the Beach Boys. They were playing. He got real bent. He made me take them off. When I turned my back, the dude copped one of my tips. The prick."

"When was he here?"

"You should have been here an hour ago. Hey, wait, he charged his food. I can get you his name." The bartender lifted up the cash drawer and went through the credit card receipts. "Yeah, here it is. The guy's name was William Stang."

"Bad habits become habits," said Slick to himself. He asked, "Did *hincky* talk about anything?"

"Dropped off a note for The Gidget"

"Is The Gidget is here?"

"Yeah, she went to the ladies room—"

"Hey sweet buns, I need another drinkie!" brayed The Gidget in a raspy voice that over the years had been cured to its fine death-rattled pitch by a combination of a three-pack-a-day cigarette habit and a steady marination of scotch. She returned to her seat, held up an empty glass and shook it. The ice cubes clinked. "Who do I have to boink to get a drink over here?"

The Gidget sat at the far end of the bar near the window. She was no longer the pristine and perky teenager with brown hair and a pony tail. She was in her late forties, and had shoulder-length, frayed, dyed-blonde hair. She had a thin figure, actually, it was more of an anorexic torque. The Gidget wore a black evening dress with a slit skirt, which advertised her long legs and artificially firm cleavage. She also wore spiked black boots with an ankle bracelet above the left foot.

"Aren't you The Gidget?" asked one of the surf club drunks, swaying.

"I'm not The Gidget, I'm a realtor, asshole," she sharply said, blowing cigarette smoke in his face. "My name is Sally Koolner."

"But you're *still* her, right?" slurred the drunk. He blinked.

"Why don't you join the rest of the pot bellies and bald spots and drink your beer?" she said, shaking her glass again. The surf club member rejoined his group. She roughly summoned the bartender. "Hit mama again with some booze, sweetcheeks."

"I see she hasn't lost her old world charm,' said Slick to the bartender.

"Yeah, the queen of skank."

"Get me her drink, please. I'll bring it over."

Joe arrived unannounced. It was nine in the evening, 1958.
There were many revealing and vulnerable things the teenage Surfer Joe wanted to say to The Gidget. He stood on the brick porch of her suburban home in The Valley. Joe was dressed in a clean shirt and pressed white pants. His hair was neatly combed. He brought a bouquet of white roses, which he stole from the rectory garden near The Bu. Joe felt uneasy. He was afraid to knock on the door. What if she rejected him? He couldn't bear it. He wanted to reveal how the sight of her walking toward him made the blood throb in his fingertips. How he was drawn to her as the ocean is to the moon. He could tell her how he just acted mean because having people mad at him kept them away. It gave him privacy. It was a way of not being hurt himself. Maybe she could help fix that. The summer was going to end soon. He wanted to go to Hawaii. Maybe she wanted to come with him. After all, why stay here? She didn't love her stepfather either. She said Mr. Koolner didn't understand why she wanted to hang out with losers at The Pit instead of the more promising men who wanted to "make something of their lives."

But before Joe knocked, he recognized The Gidget's loud and raucous laugh from the back yard. Maybe she was seeing another guy, flashed Joe. He became furious. Joe snuck along the side of the house. His barefoot sandaled feet felt the lawn's moist chill. He saw a light coming through a screen-enclosed porch in the backyard. Joe heard the metallic clicking and paper-smacking of a typewriter's keys. He stood among the lemon trees under the clear night, just beyond the illuminated swath. On the porch, Joe saw The Gidget and her stepfather. She was going through notes. He was smoking and rapidly typing in quick spurts.

"Dad, Surfer Joe is the best in The Pit. He's really the end, completely boss," said The Gidget. But she wasn't saying this, she was reading it from a piece of paper.

"I already have a publisher and an agent is already shopping around a movie deal," said Koolner, who was in his forties, had a bad toupee, wore black bifocals low on his nose, and smoked a cigarette. "I think this could be really big. Guys on the beach. A girl who wants to surf. She converts Surfer Joe from a beach bum and gets him to enroll in college. And then they get married."

The dying roses laid in the grass at the base of a lemon tree in the moonlight.

In the Malibu Boardriders Club, The Beach Boys sang on the jukebox:

> With a girl the lonely sea looks good
> Makes your night turn warm and out of sight
> Back together and do it again

"Hi, let me introduce myself, I'm Tan from the Sun," said Slick, holding out the drink to The Gidget.

"Slick," she roughly said, taking the drink and toasting him. "My savior."

"Your Dad—"

"My *step*father," she corrected, taking a sip. She shouted down the bar. "Sweetcheeks, this isn't a double scotch."

"Koolner told me—"

"I know!" peevishly said The Gidget, looking off to the dark surf. "Surfer Joe wouldn't hurt me—ever."

"How many drinks have you had?" said Slick.

"Not enough for you to look good," said The Gidget, swishing the drink around in her mouth.

The drunk loudly said to his surf club members, "Hey, I'm not shitting you, that's The Gidget."

"Everyone thinks I'm a goddamn fictional character," said The Gidget with an angry snarl to her mouth. "I never had a chance to be anything. I didn't get all of the money I deserved. My beloved stepfather gives me some, but never enough to get away. I always have to come back to him. Always." She looked off. "I lost myself."

"The same way Surfer Joe lost his thumb?" said Slick, staring at her and enjoying how the remark took away her self pity.

Fresh blood warmly spread into the foam dust on the floor of Grubby Devine's shaping room.

"Oooooooh," groaned Grubby, who might have been dying.

A few select members of The Pit Crew dragged Grubby by his one remaining limb. He left a red curved smear in the dust.

"Ooooooh," he groaned.

They dropped him beside the foam blank mold. The mold resembled a twelve-foot long by three-foot wide wooden chest with an enormous waffle iron on it. It was open. The hinged top had a concrete lid. Its insides were curved out in the shape of a surfboard. Buzzy, Kahuna, and Flippy pushed hard against the mold, tipping it over on Grubby. His head crushed with a squishy shell-cracking sound, as if he were an snail.

"You said you weren't going to hurt him," warbled Toob, shaking his head in disbelief, crying. "You were just going to blow up the place to scare him. This wasn't suppose to happen!"

"Quit it, Steak," said Koolner. "You're in this or you're on the floor with him."

"Grubby had the formula in his head," said Buzzy.

"Looks it," added Flippy, spitting on the body. "What are we going to do now? Grubby knew how to balance out the urethane. Once we have that, we can make all the foam blanks we want. Everyone will have to come to us. We don't have it."

"Joe knows where it is," said Kahuna. "He's the only one who could have convinced Grubby to try to squeeze us out."

"All the money we can make on surfboards and Joe thinks he can beat me?" Koolner said firmly. "No *surfer* ever beats me."

"We'll find him," clipped Flippy.

In the corner, a few surfboards fell, Surfer Joe sprung from behind them. His face was covered with blood and foam dust. Buzzy and Kahuna easily subdued the disabled Joe. They held him.

"You and Grubby were going to make your own blanks," Koolner said, standing before Surfer Joe.

"Please don't hurt me!" whined Joe, dropping to his knees. He blubbered, "Don't hurt me, please. I'll tell you whatever you want but don't hurt me. Please, please, please."

"Now, you're in my home break," said Koolner, picking up a tile knife from the chunks of foam on the floor. "Hold his hand."

Buzzy and Kahuna picked up the limp and sobbing Joe.

"You don't have to do this," said Toob, frightened.

"Hold his hand," ordered Koolner.

Toob reluctantly pressed Joe's hand against the over-turned mold. He said apologetically, "Joe, this is not *me* doing this."

"I said I'd tell you," Joe implored. "Please, please, don't." Tears streaked his face. Strands of elastic-like mucous tucks quivered from his nostrils. "Please."

"You're pathetic," said Koolner.

The old man hacked half of Joe's left thumb off. It made a hard snapping sound. Joe screamed. They let him go. He dropped.

"He stopped at your thumb," said Flippy, taking the knife from Koolner. "If I took off your big toe you'd never be able to surf again, I can still do that though." He flicked the knife, spattering Joe's face with blood.

"I'll give you what you want," begged said Surfer Joe, crawling on the foam-dust covered floor. "Just please don't hurt me."

Toob said, "It stops here, let him go."

"Okay," said Koolner.

Flippy picked up the bloody digit and gleefully said, "I think I'll keep this as a souvenir."

The Malibu Pit Crew smiled. Toobsteak listlessly stared at the floor and didn't bother to wipe his tears.

Fill In The Blank

The surfboard's hard shell is made from a fiberglass cloth hardened by resin and catalyst.

Within the waterproofed shell is a piece of a foam shaped like a surfboard. The shape comes from a foam blank, which is made like a giant waffle. Instead of batter, a liquid chemical is mixed with an expanding resin and poured into a surfboard-shaped mold. The mold is clamped tightly down so the growing compound can become a dense shape. A white foam blank is removed from the mold. The blank is broken lengthwise down the middle. A quarter-inch wooden strip (called a stringer) is inserted between the two halves, and the two pieces are glued back together. The stringer is the backbone of the board, without it, the surfboard would snap.

After the blank is done, a shaper lays down thin crescent strips of pasteboard on the foam blank, the strips are called templates, which are similar to sewing patterns. The shaper draws lines around the templates onto the blank to layout the exact design specifications of the board. The blank is skinned down, planed, and refined into a surfboard. The shaper has the option to airbrush colors on the blank. Once the colors are painted on the foam, and after the shaper has positioned rice paper with the his name on the blank, layers of fiberglass cloth are placed lengthwise on the shape. Resin is mixed with a catalyst chemical and brushed onto the fabric, which hardens the damp cloth into a dry durable shell.

The surf club members danced near Slick and The Gidget as the juke box kept playing the Beach Boys:

> Well I've been thinking about all the places
> We've surfed and danced
> All the faces we missed
> So let's get back together and do it again

"If Joe hates me so much, why do you think he bothered to leave this for me?" asked The Gidget, rummaging through a thickly packed purse, and pulling out a piece of crumpled paper. "See?"

Slick flattened the letter with his hand on the bar and looked at it. A spurt of ocean water came out of his nose and splattered on the note, smearing its black-marker print.

"Shit," said Slick. "Sorry, water on the brain."

"You mean water in the head."

"Hard to believe you're still single with that personality," said Slick, chugging down the beer. He put the glass down on the bar, shook the paper off, and read the smudged note:

Dearest Gidg, Gidg, Gidg...

> *We can still be what we once were. No matter what you've become I'll always know that you loved me once, and it was deep. And that is the best part of you. The part that really wanted to be a surfer girl. And you'll always be that to me. We'll always have that, and in spite of all the disappointments, we have that one moment to draw from for the rest of our lives. No one can touch that. And, in a way, that's a wonderful sweet victory. Isn't it?*

> *Love*
> *SJ*

"When you read a wave, do your lips move too?" snipped The Gidget, laughing at Slick.

"You know, there are a few words in here, I don't

understand," said Slick, glancing at the note, and feigning confusion. "What does penis-envying emasculating bitch mean?"

"Excuse me, are you really da Gidget?" slurred a drunk surf club member.

"The Gidget!" she stridently erupted. "I'm not The Gidget anymore. That's somebody else." She drained her glass and rasped out, "Another scotch—and don't water it down!"

"See ya, wouldn't want to be ya," smugly said Slick, standing up and starting to walk away, but a conversation among the surf club members caught his attention.

Five fat drunks in surf t-shirts, held beers and peered out into the surf. Slick stood at the edge of the group.

"I tell you it's Joe." said a fat drunk and balding jerk. "Surfer Joe almost took my head off. He sent my board into the beach one day, I had to do the rock dance to get it. I know that's him."

"Didn't Surfer Joe win a championship by shooting his board at somebody?"

"Johnny Slickmeyer, that's who it was, he really got ripped off," authoritatively said another member. "Slick would have been big, but the shortboard came in. And he couldn't change to the new style. Never got over it, dealt drugs and boozed too hard. He's dead now. Sixties burnout."

Slick smiled, he enjoyed seeing his life summed up by these people, and he was even happier most thought of them thought he was dead. It kept them out of his life. Slick squinted through the glass windows at the dark surf. He saw a familiar hunch-shouldered surfing silhouette come at an angle behind another rider, shoved the guy off the wave, passed by him, and effortlessly continue along the curved wall. The wave got real hollow and looked like it was going to close. But where most surfers kick out because they don't think the section ahead can be made, this particular surfer rode high, perfectly in trim. As the wave pitched, the surfer broke the parallel board free and slipped sideways down the curved shoulder, just below the crumbling foam. He beat the section. A clean sideslip. That was the giveaway. It was *too* smooth a move. You had to know the way a low tide wave was going to break that close to shore and be able to position yourself in the perfect spot to connect into the reform. And to know that, you had to anticipate what the wave was going to do. That was local knowledge. And Slick knew only two people with that much of it. Since Slick wasn't out in the water, the other person had to be: Surfer Joe.

Slick walked on the wet sand of The Bu. It was dark, but the moonlight fanned out over the beach. He could see the outline of The Wall and the bathroom. It was warm but the slight breeze felt cool. The dark mountain slopes that towered along the coastline seemed to cradle the place. Slick watched the crumbled foam of the spent waves slowly smooth out into overlapping white semi-circles on the moist brown berm. He looked back to the ocean. He noticed the swell lines wrapping further out. They were almost near the kelp line beyond the outside point. This was destined to be a huge swell. Each wave held its moving peak and peeled. Its perpetual reform was still painfully perfect. Slick leaned towards its almost magnetic pull. The waves lapped on the sand like a pulse.

"Yes my friend..."

Slick turned around. It was Joe, wearing a feather-covered hat, seal-tooth necklace a poncho, and damp surfing jams.

"I, uh, want to thank you," said Joe, clicking his cheek. "Uh."

"Thank me," abruptly said Slick, irritated. "Thank me for what?"

"For *that* wave."

"I didn't give it to you," flatly said Slick, sucking in his left cheek and slightly chewing on it. His eyes narrowed. "You still *owe* me a wave. And it's a wave that's not going to be given to me. It's a wave you'll want more than anything else and I'm going to take it."

"Payback apt," said Joe, tapping his sunglasses. "Uh."

Two huge men moved from the darkness into the moonlight.

"Who's there?" Joe distrustfully shouted, thrusting his hands into the pouch of the poncho, where he clenched an object.

"I am Rama," said one of the mysterious figures, speaking deeply.

The two turbaned strangers had sumo wrestler physiques. They wore swimming trunks and carried twelve-foot surfboards with Yin and Yang laminates in the middle of their decks.

"I am Shiva," sonorously added the other huge man.

"Here is da kine, said Rama, who smiled and added, "We like to come to Mother Bu at night to be in the water in the full moon and worship—"

"Get the hell out of my face you fucking kooks!" roared Joe, kicking sand at them. "Go back to The Valley!"

"This one is trapped in the cycle," sadly said Shama.

"Yes" said Rama, nodding. "Doomed to repeat himself."

The karmic duo departed.

Joe said, "Yes, my friend, that's one thing about this place that's never changed. The weird are still weird." He clicked his cheek and tapped his sunglasses. "But, uh, now I think they're better organized."

Slick repressed a laugh. He didn't want to be charmed.

The waves sizzled.

"So, have you seen any of the old crew?" asked Slick.

"In my own way," said Joe, his voice trailing off.

"Is there any *other* way for you?"

They looked at the waves.

"It's building," ominously said Joe, studying the ocean. "It's going to get big."

"Yeah," said Slick firmly.

"The Chumash had a phrase for a day with big waves," said Surfer Joe. "They called it a 'the day a legend dies'." He paused. "Uh, that would be the ultimate way to go out: an Aloha Wave. Disappear into all that ocean energy. Leave as one peeling and perfect spiral that opens out forever." Joe became a little edgy. "But you know what would bum me out? My board would go into shore without me, and some kook would find it, and a kook would be surfing my board." Joe clicked his cheek and paused. "I'd make sure to come back to haunt that kook."

Slick laughed; he didn't like Joe too much, but the guy was funny in a twisted sort of way.

A wave crashed on the shore; its bubbles fizzled and popped out their salty aroma.

"Aaaaah," said Joe, moving his hand in front of his nose and sniffing the air. "An excellent bouquet. Reminds me of 1955 in Malibu, a perfect year." He paused, tilting his head. "Man, 1955 was so beautiful," wistfully said Joe. "And look at this place now. The kooks ruined it. Everywhere surfers go, the kooks follow. Kooks are never at a place first. And they never have a clue to enjoy it. We knew about Hawaii. The kooks followed. We knew about Cape St. Francis. The kooks followed. We knew about Cabo. The kooks followed. Costa Rica. Kooked out. We knew about Fiji. Kooked out with hotels and dinner reservations. They destroyed everything."

"No argument," said Slick, looking down at the sand. He didn't have to clear his throat, but he did it for effect. "Koolner tried to give me two thousand bucks to find you. Why I don't know."

"Koolner is here?" harshly asked Joe, reaching back into his poncho.

"No, he wants to see—"

"Yea, yeah," said Joe, involved in another thought.

"Why did you come back?"

"What are you, a cop?" asked Joe, imitating Slick perfectly.

"Ran into The Gidget," said Slick. "She showed me—".

"Gidg...Gidg...Gidg" sputtered Joe.

The wave of pain swelled in Joe's head. It pitched and formed a liquid cylinder. Joe was back clocking time in The Black Tube. Joe crouched on his surfboard, just under the pitching lip. He felt cold. The voices within the wall of the wave shivered, "Gidget must die. Gidget must die. Gidget must die." Joe heard the thwapping sound of a surfboard. It was the approach of the dark figure. Joe turned to see the surfer's face. The shadow lunged upon him, covering him like a blanket. Joe threw it off. The Black Tube disappeared. Joe blinked at Slick.

"You all right, Joe?" asked Slick, shaking the man's shoulders.

"It's you!" Joe said accusingly, pushing Slick away. "You're the one. I should have known. You're the one!"

"Joe."

"Nothing catches me!" Joe shouted, loping toward The Wall, his necklace rattling in the darkness. "Not you or anyone!"

Slick shrugged, turned, and looked at the waves.

The surf made a grumbling sound, like a hungry stomach anticipating a meal.

From the Journal of Surfer Joe

Flippy's "Surfing World" Magazine epitomizes the conformity and industrialization of the surfing spirit. Surfing isn't a game, there is no score, and you can't sell tickets. But, Flippy knew kooks thrive in organization, competition, and status. Kooks like anything that reduces style to a predictable but stable form of expression, which enables them to package an image and sell products around it, like surfboards, wetsuits, sunglasses, clothing, whatever.

Here's how Flippy pulled it off...

A surfer gains recognition by having their picture in "Surfing

World," but to get into "Surfing World," a staff photographer must take the picture of him surfing. But to get the photographer to take that picture he must ride on a board shaped by Kahuna and wear surf merchandise manufactured by Koolner enterprises. Once the surfer gains the recognition, he's required to do well in contests, which are of course, sponsored by Surfing World and its advertisers, who are usually judges at the event. The outcome gives the surfer status as well as visibility to generate more product sales. The prefabricated surf star learns to play the promotional game for the advertisers and sponsors. He must be clean-cut, wear a tie, and blazer. He has to have a wholesome outlook by saying things like, "Surfing is great recreation for the entire family. The best part about surfing isn't winning contests, it's having fun with your friends, and sharing waves." But in real life, these surf stars are egotistical whiners and shoulder-hoping jerks who seize every wave.

Today, the total waterman who lived off the ocean has been replaced by professional surfers able to make living by being *in* the water. These surf stars aren't paddling away from the world on surfboards, they brought it into the lineup with them. They're not out to ride waves, they're trying to perfect maneuvers to get high scores in surf contests. They're not surfing, they're working. The corruption is complete.

A beach shack and a bunch of social retards had created a multi-million dollar surf industry.

"The Big One is coming to take everything with it," raved a drunk who swayed on the sidewalk.

Slick stood in the darkness. He checked out the man staggering under the streetlight by the phone stall near Malibu. The drunk held a bottle of booze in a paper sack. It was Crispy Johnson. Crispy still wore the silver 'Windandsea' jacket and the same heavily rumpled and stained bluejeans. He was shirtless and barefoot. Slick didn't want to talk to Crispy when he was wasted. He stayed in the shadows, hoping his drunk friend would drift away. But then, Slick saw Purpus running down the sidewalk.

"The Big One is going to come!" shouted the angry man. "It's all—"

"You seen Slick?" asked Purpus.

"What do I look like, a dictionary?" growled Crispy.

"I was suppose to meet him for a beer at the Boardriders Club," said Purpus. "The bartender told me he came down here."

"Hey," Slick said, walking out into the light.

"That's a cool bar back there, they play the Beach Boys," enthusiastically said Purpus. "The Beach Boys got me into surfing. Seemed like a great place. Everybody was having fun, drinking and dancing. You know the Beach Boys are going to be playing at the contest, I'm looking forward to see—"

Purpus stopped, he noticed Slick and Crispy exchange looks and shake their heads. Skip felt he had done or said something uncool.

"You're the writer guy, Slick's bro. He told me about you," said Crispy, hawking mucous and spitting it out with a sharp snap. "You been surfing your whole life?"

"No, only a couple months back East to try to get in shape," said Purpus, shrugging, a little embarrassed.

"And you're old."

Purpus took the statement the way anyone else his age would. He said,"Thirty-eight."

"You're dooooomed," said Crispy, peering into Purpus and studying him closely. The drunk's eyes widened in recognition. "You're stoked. Looked at him Slick, your kook is stoked!" Crispy laughed; it turned into a hacking cough. "There's no going back for you now. Once you get stoked, surfing's all you want to do. When you're a kid you have the time to do it, but when you're an adult, you have to give up everything." Crispy tucked the bottle under his arm and clapped. "When you get that first taste, it's like a fire inside you, you can't put it out with water, water just keeps it going. It just makes you thirstier. The stoke consumes you. Burns you out." Crispy laughed. "You're a doomed man."

"I'm use to that, I grew up in New Jersey."

"Sorry," said Slick.

They listened to the waves sizzling, sounding as if a giant molten object had just been shoved into the ocean to cool off.

"He missed out, didn't he, Slick?" knowingly said the drunk, smiling with his yellowish red-lined teeth.

"You use to light up those waves, Crispy," said Slick.

"Yeah, I accelerated out there," said Crispy, deeply snorting mucous back into this nasal passages, as if he were storing it.

"Yeah, you did," said Slick, nodding.

"What can I do now, anyway?" said Crispy in a maudlin

tone. "Is someone going to hire me to sleep under the pier? Sweep up a surf shop? What can I do? No one will pay me to do what I do." He paused. "What can I do?"

Slick looked at Crispy and shook his head. It was hard to believe those thin arms were once thick and bulging, and how his cobblestone walk of stomach muscles had eroded away to a shapeless path that lead to nowhere. In the late forties and throughout the fifties, Crispy lived off the ocean and surfed Malibu every day in the Spring to the end of September. He had the lifestyle of a millionaire, while guys confined in itchy suits worked away their vibrant years and hoped to enjoy a similar lifestyle in their retirement. When Crispy's surf crew walked off the beach to college, a job, marriage, or death (In 1954, Simmons died on an eight-foot day at a break called Windandsea in La Jolla.), Crispy lost the line-up of his world. He didn't want to leave the beach. But, he couldn't live the kook life. And his Malibu was gone. In the sixties, he played in a band, and surfed, and dealt drugs, but he made the mistake of becoming his best customer. Booze and drugs gave him a world where he could live in between the loss of Malibu and the reality of choosing an entry level position in the kook world. Crispy stayed that way. He enjoyed the view.

"You just had too much fun," said Slick.

Crispy proudly growled, "Goddamn right I did."

Purpus said, "It must have been fun—"

"You should have seen the ocean back then," ruefully said Crispy. He smiled. The deep wrinkles on his face wrapped like swell lines around his eyes. "It was a real ocean—not this piss-hardon ocean. It was a surfer's ocean. The waves were different. Better. You think this place is perfect? Sheeet. It's changed. It was more perfect then. What we had was really perfect. Now the waves are just different. Too much buildings and shit, the dickwads fucked the coastline all up with seawalls, oil-drilling platforms, jetties, marinas, piers...all that shit built up over the years. Man, it just shifted the sand around, messing with what nature does best. People say it hasn't changed, but they're the ones who don't notice. I was there, *there.* I'm there. And here, I can see it, I can see the change." Crispy narrowed his eyes, and looked warily at the night, as if "they" were coming. He defiantly added, "I'm glad I got my waves. I got more than my share before the damn Gidget shit. All those crowds now, you'd never get me out there, I'm not going to bang my head on that wall. We need The Big One to clean up the whole beach, man. A huge surnami, one of those big Jap waves, come right in, take out all those asswipes off the hills." He hawked mucous, spit with a snap, and sighed. "God, this place was *so* bitchen."

"We're going to get something to eat," said Slick, who had heard all of Crispy's rants.

"Hey," said Crispy in a conspiratorial tone to Slick. "Can you spare a few bucks for some suds? I know, I know I owe you ten, but I'm good for it. I'll get you back." He smiled. "You're the only one who's always been good to me. You know I'll get you back."

Slick reached into his pocket and handed Crispy a five.

"God bless you, bro," said Crispy, loudly snorting mucous.

Two attractive girls in halter tops and shorts strutted down the sidewalk toward the men. The girls' eyes were flat. They didn't want to acknowledge anyone.

"Hello ladies," courtly said Crispy. "Can I interest you in a wrist corsage?"

The girls stopped.

Crispy's quite impressive penis was hanging out of his open fly and draped over his wrist.

Purpus and Slick laughed. The girls said nothing, stared ahead, and quickly dug their heels like hooves into the concrete and cantered away.

"You toads!" sourly yelled Crispy after the girls. He calmed down. "The girls then were different too. That move use to get me laid a lot." Crispy tucked his member back into his pants, but didn't zip it up. "I'm tired of being everybody's escapegoat. Let it all go to hell. The Big One is coming! The Big One is coming!"

Slick and Purpus waved and walked away. They looked back. Crispy swayed, stuck his chest out, and strutted down the sidewalk. He ranted at his unseen enemy. He tried to call it out. No one appeared to take him on. Suddenly, as if in answer to Crispy's challenge, a distant crumbling rumble came from the sea, sounding like an artillery barrage from a nearby destroyer. A huge wave closed out in the far off darkness way beyond the outside reef. The entire ocean became an apron of white foam advancing to shore, looking like a stampede of sheep.

"What's out there?" said Slick, taken aback.

"The Big One is coming, Slick," eagerly chattered Crispy, swaying and looking into the dark ocean. "It's just roaming. Just roaming."

Koolner aimed the unloaded Mannilicher Carcano. Its stock was weather worn and slightly porous. The rifle's leather strap was thin and scuffed. The old man sat at his desk chair. Koolner pointed the gun toward the waves. As if he were back reliving a moment, the old man rapidly pulled the bolt action a few times and squeezed off the trigger for each imaginary shot. He looked at his watch and said to himself, "Three shots in 5.6 seconds." He smiled, looked off, and sighed. "Memories."

The phone on his desk rang. It was Flippy. He was furious at Koolner.

"You better be having this place watched," shouted Flippy. "I feel like a minnow on a hook in a shark cage."

"I know Joe's coming."

"So what good does that do me?"

"Hey Stinker's, no!" commanded Koolner, hitting the black box's button. The dog yelped from an electric shock in its collar. The old man tried to calm Flippy down. "When Joe comes in they will take care of him. There's nothing to worry about."

"I'd feel better if *you* were sitting here," evenly said Flippy. "Why do I have to be in my office?"

"So Joe won't know we suspect anything. If we're going to trap him, Flip, you have to be vulnerable," said Koolner. "Just stall him. Provoke him. He'll start to rant. He'll get off—Stinker's no!" The dog yelped from an electric shock.

"Just cover my ass if you want yours covered," clipped Flippy into the phone. He nervously spun back and forth in his swivel chair. The surf publisher was so caught up in his irritation, he didn't even notice the figure moving behind him.

"Hey, if it wasn't for me, you'd be fighting bums for empties in trash cans at the beach!" said Koolner. "Get down from there!" A dog yelped and cried again. "Later." The phone clicked.

"Yeah," said Flippy, slamming down the phone. "And if it wasn't for you I wouldn't be rich and worried about some Malibu-ized surfer wanting to kill me because I was in a fucking Gidget movie."

Surfer Joe pressed a sharp tomahawk-shaped fin against the publisher's throat.

"Yes, my friend. Time to get happy," said Joe, standing behind Flippy like a barber ready to give a seated man a shave. "Uh, let's bury the hatchet fin."

Surfer Joe paced back and forth in front of Flippy. He tapped the flat side of the fin into his left palm. Flippy sat behind his desk. His wrists bound with duct tape to the armrests of his chair.

"Yes, my friend...now, since you don't surf anymore," said Surfer Joe, musing aloud. "Since you have no need to surf, I couldn't cut off your big toe. Since you don't write anymore, I couldn't really accomplish anything by cutting off your thumbs. Now, what can I cut off? Something that you can *still* do?"

"You're an asshole, you've always been an asshole," flatly snapped Flippy. "Pretty tough now, aren't you? You whiney sack of shit. Big goddamn little baby."

"Yes, the verdict is in," declared Joe, pointing his thumbless nub at the publisher. "You're guilty."

"Guilty of what?"

"Guilty of turning surfing into a sport," spat Joe, pounding his fist on the desk. "Surfing isn't a sport. Surfing is a journey, a path, a quest. Only a kook would call it a sport." Joe tilted his head and tapped his sunglasses, and swung his arms around. His seal tooth necklace clicked. He started speaking rapidly. "Did you ever hear anyone say, 'I baseball through life?' 'I basketball through life?' No, but when you say 'I surf through life,' it means something. I've proven style over substance is superior. Substance exists without style, but it's just substance—it's dead. Style gives substance meaning."

"Asshole, asshole, asshole," mockingly sang Flippy. "Save that bullshit for the magazines." He spoke in baby talk. "Did wittle Joey wose his wittle home bweak?" He grumbled. "Well, kiss my ass and make it better!"

"You're guilty of more than that my redundant friend!" raged Joe, ripping off a black-and-white photo from the wall. "Ruining Rincon: Guilty!" He tore down another picture. "Ruining Trestles: Guilty!" As Joe continued his indictment, he ripped several frames off the wall and named each surf spot. "Swamis and Huntington and Doheny and San Onofre: Guilty! Guilty! Guilty! and, Guilty! Anytime there was a new spot, you'd show up, bankrolling Corky, and have a surf film made, and nothing was left. Nothing." He paused, clicked his cheek, looked upward and said,"Uh, wait a second, Daddy-o, I like think I'm having an epiphany."

Flippy listened. He didn't hear anyone coming. Where were Koolner's boys? He had to get Joe going again on a rant.

"How come I'm guilty? You're in those pictures Joe."

"You would have taken them anyway," said Joe. "All I wanted to do was just surf."

"Always the exception never the rule, huh?" coolly said Flippy, shaking his head and laughing. "No one cares anymore about who is the King of Malibu, don't you get it? No one! The only people who remember you are over forty. Young people don't even know you, don't even care about you. Your legend, your myth, no one cares!" He snorted. "And, being King of Malibu just meant you were the biggest dick in the water. No one liked you ever. Slick is the real king. He was king of The Pit because everyone respected him. He shared waves. He had and still has a better style. You couldn't hang on the beach because you burned so many people in the water everyone hated you on the beach. You never had any friends, ever."

"I think I'll keep this as a souvenir," said Joe, picking up the paperweight.

"You humped her," defiantly accused Flippy. "She fooled you, you were in love with The Gidget—"

"Gidg...Gidg...Gidg..." Joe sputtered.

Joe pulled into The Black Tube. It cooed like a passionate lover, "Gidget must die, Gidget must die, Gidget must die." Joe heard the slapping surfboard again. The dark surfer was even closer now. He was going to run over Joe. Joe couldn't let this happen. He screamed and jumped out toward the opening in the tube and found himself dry and standing by Flippy.

"Surf's up," Joe soothingly said, slashing down the razor sharp fin.

The unconscious Flippy lost a lot of blood in the next two hours. He sat behind his desk. A round cake of surf wax was shoved in his mouth. His suit was soaked a dark brown. Flies buzzed and flitted around the publisher. He slowly awoke. The pain throbbed in his body. It blurred his vision. He squinted. He saw the newly resined paperweight. It was an eight-ounce size Dixie-cup shape placed at the center of his desk. Flippy tried to scream but it came out a muffled hum.

Preserved in resin, positioned upright for all time, was a Flippy's penis.

"Say Phrancky, he's still alive!"

"Yeah, who knew?" indifferently replied her partner.

Flippy saw women enter the office. At least one of them seemed like a woman. Weren't they going to untie him? How come they weren't shocked? It was as if they expected to find him this way.

"Mmmmmmm," he squeezed out. His eyes tearing.

Annette approached the man. He expectantly looked up. She took out a clear plastic bag and put it over Flippy's head. She tied it tightly around his neck. Flippy jerked. He couldn't tip the chair over. He was too weak. The cake of surf wax in his mouth prevented him from chewing through the bag, which was becoming hot and sticky with sweat. He sucked hard against the plastic, but his nostrils couldn't draw any air. He struggled. Through the cloudy plastic he saw the two women watch him. They seemed bored.

Annette and Phrancky impassively studied the man with the plastic-wrapped sucking head.

"We'll never make the restaurant before it closes," glumly said Annette, looking at her watch.

Phrancky tossed her head and shook her long, dyed blonde hair, smiled and said, "Hey, the dickless wonder is finally fading."

Flippy slumped forward

Annette cockily swaggered to the desk, picked up the phone and dialed a number.

"Hello." said the voice on the other end.

"I *wanted* to talk to him first," Phrancky said, stamping the floor with her spiked heels.

"He's wiped out," said Annette to her boss. "Forever."

"Do you always have to take control of every situation?" whined Phrancky.

"Shuttup," loudly snapped Annette, covering the phone's mouthpiece with her hand. "Who's next? Kahuna?"

"I'd say so," said Koolner. His voice followed by a click and a dial tone.

"You're welcome," said Annette, hanging up the phone.

Phrancky picked up the fiberglass member and said, "It's still warm."

"That's mine," said Annette, grabbing for it.

"You broke my nail," said Phrancky, pulling Annette's nose ring.

"Aaaaaaaah!" yelled Annette, blood spurting from her nostril. She viciously yanked Phrancky's hair. Phrancky dropped the object. The two women wrestled to the floor in front of the desk.

The dead man's eyes blankly looked at the paperweight, which wobbled on its round bottom edge like a dying top.

It was the last mansion on the hills Joe wired for destruction.

"Back in time," softly cooed Joe, stealthily working under Koolner's outside widow's walk.

Joe wrapped the last of several greenish PETN datasheets around the pilings. The rubber-like datasheets were an inch-and-one-quarter thick and six-inches wide, and four feet in length. One sheet was equal to ten pounds of dynamite and could destroy your average house. Each of the sheets was connected by a primacord fuse. He didn't have much primacord left, but he didn't want to risk using an extinguishable fuse on Koolner's place. Joe was ready for the next step, he took a few quarter-pound sticks of dynamite, taped them together, and awled out the center with a pair of blunt-nosed pliers. Once this was done, he inserted his last safety fuse into the cigarette-tube shaped plastic blasting cap, and crimped them together with the pliers. Joe wrapped the dynamite at the base of the porch's piling and covered the sticks with gravel. He decided to add dynamite to the mix because it was a better worker, it really ripped things apart. Joe even hung a few two-gallon gas cans to add fire, which would increase the irreparable damage of the blast (a two-gallon can of gas equals fourteen sticks of dynamite) He secured the cans with bailing wire to the posts. He didn't want them to bang around. Joe had done this to eight of the twelve pilings. Finally, Joe took an antenna-mounted receiver he constructed from a car alarm, and placed it in some brush to conceal it. The receiver was programmed to a specific radio frequency. All Joe had to do was press one button on a transmitter, and send out the radio wave to the receiver. The signal to the receiver would close the switch, causing the capacitor to dump its energy, sparking the primacord and safety fuses into the blasting caps, which were wedged into the datasheets and dynamite. And then...

All the bungalows with their precious mean high-tide property lines.

"Booooom." Joe whispered.

All the multi-million dollar mountain and hilltop mansions that overlooked The Bu.

"Boooooooom."

Every overpriced hotel, souvenir shop, boutique, fast-food franchise, ocean-view restaurant, t-shirt booth, surf shops, and supermarkets.

"Booooooooooooooom."

The Malibu pier and the Malibu Boardriders Club.

"Booooooooooooooooooooom."

Joe planned to press the transmitter's detonation button on his Aloha Wave at The Gidget Longboard Invitational. The Beach Boys were suppose to play at the event. Maybe, Joe thought, The Beach Boys will be there at the time of the blast. That would be *choice*. But, destroying Malibu and killing The Beach Boys was too much to hope for, Joe concluded, after all, he had to be realistic.

The dark figure of a one-legged pelican hobbled along the berm to the moonlit waves. The bird's wings were frayed. A rusty fishing hook was embedded in one of its leg welts. The pelican's left eye was half closed. There were remnants of oil and sludge on its feathers. The bird had bald spots splotched with infected open sores. The beat creature just made it to the lapping water, and paddled out a few feet. But the waves in the shorebreak smacked into the struggling bird and washed the lopsided pelican back. Slowly, the pelican righted itself, and went toward the ocean again. This time the disoriented bird managed to swim out just a bit. Its head lolling a little. Another wave hit. The bird ducked into the water but it didn't resurface. A small, limp, feathered body washed back on the wet and tightly packed sand. The pelican lay there. Wave after wave lifted the bird and pushed it onto drier sand. Then, as the tide slowly rose, the feathered body finally tumbled back to its Malibu.

Chapter five

Pumping

It was classic Malibu. And it was going off. This was the first taste of a solid swell. And it was going off. The incoming tide just covered the rock-stubbled shore. The lines stacked as they hit the first outside reef. Line after line after line. The place was on fire. The waves scooped out at four to six feet. They zippered in a grinding spiral from the outside point for a quarter mile to shore without sectioning. It was firing. The breaking waves looked like giant fuses, incinerating themselves into a powdery mass. It was really going off. And it was clean. The surface was glassy. The shoulders had schools of silvery speckles flashing across their thin turquoise faces. Maximum glitter. A reforming gem. Wind feathered the tips and a line of sunlight brushed a soft blue trim beneath its edge. This was a painting you could surf. You could go off with its colors. It was going off. You could go off with it.

"Look at that!" shouted Purpus, moving from one foot to the other, amped, Jones-ing like a junkie.

"Fuck it, The Juice isn't worth the squeeze, bro," glumly said Slick, placing his board against The Wall. "It's a fiberglass curtain out there. I'd just be a burn victim in another wave of hell."

The word had gotten out to The Valley. It was five-thirty in the morning but already there were two hundred and twenty surfers in the water. It looked as if there was a shipwreck, and the survivors were clinging to debris to stay afloat. There were screams, collisions, and twelve people on the wave.

"Let's charge it." said Purpus. "It's bitchen."

"You go," said Slick, indifferently staring at the crowded ocean. "Six-foot waves and fifteen assholes to a wave. No one can turn. No one can cut back. That's a special pocket out there. There's only enough room to make the right move to properly surf it." He paused. "I don't like the aggro vibe. Too intense. It's like a day without any surf to me."

"It's *still* Malibu."

"It's there, somewhere, underneath all that."

"Well, give me a little hoot, okay?" said Purpus, laying down his board. He unraveled the ten-foot long, quarter-inch wide, urethane plastic cord which was wound around the board's tail and fin. He put the cord's Velcro strap around his ankle.

"You're wearing a kook cord!" derisively said Slick. "Only dog's wear leashes!"

"Woof! Woof!" said Purpus, smirking and running out toward the surf. "It's better than swimming."

Slick glared at the surfer-impacted waters. He knew what was out there. All those kooks hassling and trying to out position each other. Clawing around each other. It was as if they weren't out there to surf. They yelled and screamed for a wave like stockbrokers shouting for bids on an exchange floor. They enjoyed beating each other out for something. They liked depriving someone else of a pleasure. The whole time these kooks rode a wave, they twisted their mean faces in glum snarls. They glared like they could evaporate you with their gazes. During their rides, they territorial swung their boards around to drive everyone back. They weren't surfing the wave, they were guarding it. Slick didn't want to fight it today. He didn't want to become their world. He just wanted to surf. He had Malibu on so many good days. Let the kooks beat each other. But the crowd didn't stop Surfer Joe...

Amid the swimming swarm, Slick easily spotted him. Joe always prone paddled with his left leg bent and his foot up in the air. He stroked for an outside wave with eight others around him. As the wave pitched, Joe dropped from the peak, but faded a little to his left. He brought the board around in a wide roundhouse cutback into a teenager's face. The board crushed the punk's nose like a peach. The shortboarder fell behind Joe and collided into three surfers. There was no joy in Joe's movements. There was a calibrated vengeance. Joe gleefully ran over anyone lying in his path. A surfer dropped in front of him, Joe nimbly stepped on the nose of the kook's board, pushing its tip underwater, and bucking the rider off it. Another intruder dropped in. Joe pushed the kook off his board. Another uninvited guest dropped in. Joe grabbed a surfer's leash cord and viciously yanked the kook from his board. Another surfer was trying to paddle over the face. Joe ran him over and cruised into the reforming wave. Joe saw a man swimming in the ocean, holding a camera in a waterproof-housing. Joe put all his weight on the tail, lifting the board halfway out of the water, and brought it down, slamming the bottom of the forty-pound balsa board on the photographer's head, knocking him out.

"No pictures!" said Surfer Joe, eyes aglow, thriving in the fiberglass carnage.

Joe continued to work the crowd, effortlessly slaloming through the logjam of surfers who sat or paddled in the water. Surfboards flew about the air around Joe. The vanquished offenders were swept to shore in the white water behind him. Joe didn't even look. He didn't care. The kooks were trying to take *his* wave. He turned left to the curl. Ahead the shoulder began to hollow out. He brought the board around and rode parallel against the rising face. He streaked in perfect trim, a flat thin wake of foam behind the tail, like a vapor trail. Joe was locked into the power pocket, just barely ahead of the curl. He crouched with his arms straight out in front of him. The wave's lip combed over his right shoulder, creating a slight cavern behind him. Joe resembled a caveman with his hands over an imaginary fire. The wave tapered down. Joe stood and cross stepped backwards to the tail. He dropped his right knee and cutback. The tapered wall started to rise again into a bluish-green escarpment, as if it were a cape unfurling from his board. Joe's style seemed smooth to most, but Slick detected a strained and forced quality to his maneuvers. Joe appeared skittish. His slouch looked like a disappointed slump. Joe didn't seem to be walking the board. He was pacing it, as if he felt confined on it, trapped in his style.

"My waves! My waves! My waves!" Joe triumphantly yelled.

Joe extended his right arm, held out his hand, curled in its lower three fingers, pointed the next digit out, and stuck his thumb up. He aimed the pointed finger at surfers floating in the water, as if the extended digit was a barrel and the thumb was the hammer of a tiny pistol, and he was shooting them down. In the shallows, the wave's shoulder crumbled into slushy foam. Joe banked off it to shore. He stepped onto the beach. The board beside him came to a grating stop in the sand. A grim platoon of shortboarders was waiting for him.

"You dick!" shrieked a bloody-faced teenager with a broken nose. "You're going to die."

"So are you, but with a fucking ugly nose," said Joe.

The punk was reinforced by teenagers with buzzcuts, who had all been victims of Joe's surfing style. They surrounded him.

"You're amoebas in a cesspool," mockingly said Joe, giving a stink-eyed look to the shortboarders.

"Wolf pack him," commanded the one with the broken nose.

"Kooks!" Joe wailed.

The shortboarders started pounding Surfer Joe. He had no chance to get off his knees.

"Hey," shouted Slick, parting through the angry wave of teenagers with his longboard. "Back off." Slick commanded.

The punks pulled away.

"You again!" snarled the broken-nosed teenager.

Slick smiled, it was the same Rasta Head whose board he destroyed the day before. Boy, was this kid getting an education.

"Well," said Slick, looking at the Rasta punk and the buzzcutters, "If it isn't the new group, Jah and the Testicle Heads."

"Fuck off," said Rasta Head.

"You're cursed, cursed by the Chumash," shouted Joe getting up from the sand. "You come out of the ocean the same way you came in. That's your punishment. That's your curse—"

The broken-nosed teenager ran at Joe and cleanly hit him in the head with a flying kick, dropping Joe to his knees.

"Asshole!" Rasta Head bravely said, running away.

The sun tasered into Joe's eyes. A driving pain throbbed deep in his skull. It was so intense he dropped to his knees. The sizzling of the waves sounded like static. The blackness disappeared. He was in a field of white splinters. The static broke apart. The pain's wave carried Joe up its rising face and deposited him on the shore, as if he were a shell. He was back into a clear, warm Malibu day. And bleeding. It was an *altered* Joe who was back...

"No, no, no! Kooks! The valleys, the valleys, they're here!" keened Joe, looking around at the packed beach and the overdeveloped hills and the traffic-clogged Coast Highway. "What are these short boards! Where's Toob's shack? Where's Malibu? Where's my Malibu?" He looked with horror at his hand. "My fucking thumb!"

"He's gonzo, man," said one of the testicle heads.

"Yeah, a burnout," said another buzzcut, laughing and wandering away with his friend.

"Hey," said a concerned Slick, leaning over Joe.

"Slick, you're old man," gasped Joe. "You must be at least thirty!"

"Joe!"

"I fooled you, Slick," said Joe, his flat gaze became alert and focused. He wagged a finger at him, laughing.

Slick's eyes narrowed, he clenched his right hand and said, "That seemed a little too real for even you to be faking."

"It's not my Malibu anymore," spluttered Joe, standing up. He lurched off with his forty-pound board. "I owned this place, now I'm just in the way."

"No argument," said Slick, shouting after Joe. "Don't bother thanking me for helping you. You Ass—"

"Asshole!"

Slick turned to the surf.

"Asshole!" shouted a kook at the surfer in front of him, nudging the nose of his board on the guy's tail.

"Learn to surf I'll get out of you're fucking way!" yelled back the kook, turning his board to drive the guy back.

"Asshole!"

Slick watched the two kooks surfing on a wave near the shore. Both surfers were way ahead of the curl, out of the concept. They kept yelling at each other, "Asshole...dickhead...Fuck you...Move shithead." Neither one was in the right spot of the wave, but they were so intent on yelling at each other, they didn't notice. Finally, one leapt off his board and tackled the other from behind. Their surfboards collided with a flat thump and loud cracking sound. The two grown men thrashed in the water and screamed, "Shit......Fuck you..."

The succulently peeling Malibu wave obliviously continued without them to the shore, undemanding, indifferent, and perfect.

Slick admired the flawless wave and gloomily wondered why something so beautiful could bring out so much ugliness in people?"

Phrancky aimed the Mannlicher Carcano. It wasn't hard to find the target. The sight's cross hairs were centered over Surfer Joe's right nipple. An easy kill shot.

"I could waste him now," grunted Phrancky, standing on the patio deck, leaning against the railing, and leveling the rifle. She tracked Joe. He walked to the public shower outside the bathroom. "Hey, the scope is off."

"You're underestimating this weapon," said Koolner, gently taking the rifle, and gazing upon it like a child he just gave birth to. "I bought it years ago from a mail order house, American Rifleman, I think. It's 6.5 mm, has a four-power scope. It has a low kick, which helps rapid firing. The bullets are heavier. You can use full-jacketed shells. Travel like an AK-47, 2,100 feet per second. Thing only weighs eight pounds, has three pounds of pull."

"So what?"

"It kinda has sentimental value," said Koolner, taking up the rifle and looking through the scope at Joe. "Man, it would be so easy, but...he's not *finished* yet."

"If you kill Surfer Joe now you don't have to worry about him coming after you."

"Joe, after me?" asked Koolner in a harsh tone. "Surely, that's an occurrence you don't plan on happening."

"No," blurted Phrancky, feeling self-conscious. "But what if I miss with that rifle? You can't hit anything with this piece of shit."

"It came in real handy for me once," said Koolner, aiming at Joe and pulling the trigger on the unloaded rifle.

Joe stood on the concrete walkway that went around the municipal bathroom's outside shower. It was one of three narrow spray-nozzles six feet up on the gray cinder-brick wall. He turned it on. He rinsed the blood off his face with cold water.

"'Surfer Joe lives'," said Crispy, reading the words on the Malibu Wall and urinating on them.

Joe grinned, toweling off. He put on his sunglasses and he said, "Yes, my friend, you're looking good."

"Over the years, it's amazing how much better looking we've gotten," answered Crispy, staring down and urinating. "You know you're old when you have an erection and you don't have to push it down to take a whiz."

Joe laughed. His face changed. He seemed carefree.

"A lot of time gone by, things just get longer," observed Joe.

"Like our rap sheets," said Crispy who finished, tucked, but didn't zip up.

Joe laughed. They looked at the waves.

"It's peeling today, Joe, spiraling," Crispy said, sticking out a finger and rolling it around in tight circles. "It's coming up. It's building into something." He squinted. "Your head dinged?"

"Yeah, cold cocked by a kook."

"That's why he's a kook," said Crispy, hiccoughing. "If I had my good boots on and saw the dude who did it to you I'd take that son of a bitch out. Shit, I'll fire up that brick." He glared at the beach crowd. "They ought to just drop a bomb on this whole place and start all over."

Crispy took out a white handkerchief, unfolding and placing it beneath his nose. He poked his cloth-covered finger into his left nostril, and twisted it around. He pulled out the handkerchief and examined its contents.

"Looking for brain matter?" asked Joe.

"Not going to find much of that," said Crispy, chuckling with a wheeze. He snorted and leveled a sharp look at Joe. "I'm surprised you show your face around here." Crispy used the nosepicking technique on the other nostril. "You're lucky Slick helped you, he of all people should have joined in to kick your ass." He paused. "You stole Slick's chance Joe. Slick's a better surfer than you."

"Yes, but he has no mystique," replied Joe, clicking his cheek, slouching his body, and acting like he was riding a wave.

"You're a legend in your own mind," said Crispy, putting the handkerchief away.

Joe's grin turned into a grim straight line. His eyes flared and he said, "I hate that, look at that."

Purpus didn't want the larger waves. He tried that yesterday, but he didn't even get a chance. Every time he paddled for a wave, somebody loudly swore at him, and Skip would pull out. It was too intimidating. Too much competition. He wanted no part of that—it would be like work. If he was going to have to fight that hard for something and get that aggravated, he'd be doing it for money not rides to the beach. Skip wanted to have fun. Today, he simply contented himself to sit inside, closer to shore. Maybe, he might pick off quick rides on waves no one else wanted. He got his chance.

It was a smaller wave, but the better surfers went over it for a bigger one. Slick furiously spun around and paddled, his hands smacking and splashing the water, his body moving side to side, rocking the board. His head straight down on the deck. Then, he felt an energy beside his own force pushing the board forward, lifting and tipping it downward. He caught the wave! Purpus glided diagonally across the face. He slowly did a combination push-up and squat thrust to get his legs under him. He stood bent and stiff with his arms out in a karate move. His feet wide apart. He cautiously shuffled two steps forward. Down the line ahead of him, he saw the three-foot high wave sucking out. The wind bowled it into a bluish green pod. He rode into it. The pod's feathered-tipped edges flared out like white spikes, curled and held like an eave over his head. He was within the living swirl. Light burned through the back of the wave. Purpus struggled to keep his balance. The lip pitched, slicing down and coolly plashing on his shoulders and chest, covering him with effervescent foam. He only saw white. He tasted salt. Purpus bent down like he'd seen surfers do in photographs, then he grabbed the outside rail for support. The white water lessened its force. His vision cleared. He saw the curved valley of the shoulder ahead of him, rising. But, the curl overtook him and foam swept the board out from under his feet. Purpus rolled underwater until the wave released him. He pressed his feet on the rocky bottom and pushed up.

"Owwwwwww!" Purpus howled, bursting through the surface. His heart pumped rapidly. He felt as if the ride rearranged his molecular structure. He was stoked. Baptized. Charged. His eyes were glazed and gleamed. A long dormant pilot light flamed up in his head. He looked outside at the lines of waves still coming in. The shape of each wave mesmerized him. Its dynamics were awesome. The wave wasn't the water moving forward—it's the shape of the energy as it moves *through* the ocean. Yes, that's what Purpus rode—that force, that Juice. He connected with it. He wanted to be plugged within it again. Skip believed the water was a solution that would bring out the best in him. Skip could grow and develop from its force. It was like living an entirely different life. He wanted it. The Juice could change him. Purpus sloppily paddled toward that life.

"God I hate that!" Joe hissed, pointing at Skip's ride. "Can you believe that shit? A kook getting an inside wave all to himself!" Joe, wove his hands about more and more rapidly as his rant accelerated. "The kook even howled. Kooks don't surf, they *stand*. They just turn around and paddle out for another one, back and forth. They're not surfers, they're commuters. They miss it. The pointillism, uh, is lost. Kooks see a mountain, an avalanche, they don't see the secret within the pattern of the spiral, the helix, the unrolling perpetual horizon of another world. They miss it, man." He clicked his cheek. "A Malibu wave has to be earned."

"It's a total Valley takeover. The kooks own the hills, the beach, and rule the ocean, there's nothing you can do," despondently responded Crispy, sipping a cocktail-in-a-can drink. "Look at all this federales' control freak stuff." He pointed to a sign.

Joe gave the sign a withering glance:

No alcohol
No fishing
No swimming
No camping
No running
No fires
No Frisbee
No ballplaying
No shouting
No dogs
No barbecuing
No littering
No kayaking
No glass containers
No skimboarding
No nudity
No loitering

"No loitering," said Joe, scoffing in disbelief. "You could get arrested for loitering by just standing here and trying to read everything on the goddamn sign."

"You got that right," said Crispy, starting to get the gleam of a drunken glare in his eyes. "They're surveilling us."

"You know what our problems was Crispy," said Joe, tilting his head and tapping his fingers to his sunglasses. "We were too cool." He paused. "Uh, we're victims of style."

"You think so, huh," said Crispy, hawking up some mucous and spitting it out with a whip-cracking snap. "You can't even see to the bottom of the water anymore. There's no growth on the rocks. Sometimes when I'm looking at this place, I can't tell if it's breaking or just trying to flush itself out." He paused. "Some days it stinks like shit. I mean you smell *real* shit."

Joe spoke the next words slowly and softly, "I found a Malibu, Crispy. I found a place where it's Malibu all the time...Follow me."

Koolner showed her the turd from his treatment plant. The piece of dehydrated sludge reflected on the old man's huge mirrored sunglasses. They looked like crinkled pupils.

"Go ahead, smell it," proudly said Koolner, holding up the processed human sludge by Annette's nose.

"I'll pass," Annette said, cringing. Her face curled in disgust.

"It's odorless," said Koolner, sniffing it. "It's like a wood chip."

"I said I'll pass."

The old man flicked the dried waste away. It landed into a stream of treated water and floated down to the Malibu Creek's rivermouth. He looked above at the two-hundred condominiums he built in the hills. The development was called "The Colony." All the units were wood-shingled, and perched precariously on an incline. The treatment plant processed the condo's waste. The plant had a series of large round tanks placed in a descending order on the slope. It was a gravity system. The round tanks were evenly spaced thirty feet apart in a descending order. They were twenty-feet high and had a fifty-foot diameter. Their sides were covered with ivy. The top two tanks contained raw sludge, the next few dealt with processing, aerating, and then flowed into a settling pond, where anything left over would be processed again.

"Let me give you the grand tour," said the denture-clicking Koolner to Annette.

They walked past a barb-wire tipped cyclone fence that contained construction equipment, lumber, and several ten-foot high stacks of twelve-foot long plastic chutes.

"What's with that stuff?" asked Annette, pointing to the chutes.

"A fuck up," said Koolner, laughing. "I wanted to build a

waterslide, but the Bakersfield shitheads wouldn't let me."

"God," said Annette, attempting to breathe through her mouth. "How can you stand the smell at this place?"

"You want to see something that really stinks?" excitedly tittered Koolner, bounding up the steeper incline until he reached the ladder on the lowest of the two raw sludge tanks at the top of the hill. "I'll show you something that stinks!" He clambered up the ladder. "Come on, don't let an old man like me show you up."

"All these flies," groaned Annette, slapping them away and climbing up behind Koolner, who had a money-packed wallet protruding from his back pocket.

"These two top towers are where all the honey goes," delightfully said Koolner, giggling. The old man stood on a metal-grill platform. He pulled her up to his side. She looked down at the steel-domed tank. Koolner hit a button. There was an electronic hum, followed by a metallic scrapping noise. The door on the top of the tank slid open part way. Koolner hit the button again. The doors stopped. Annette saw the percolating black sludge. It simmered with heat waves. Bugs coated the waste like moving dark sprinkles on fudge. Annette saw huge green-shelled insects with plump black bodies and numerous legs. The smell was horrible, but the sight of the repulsive, gluttonous, and luxuriating bugs somehow made it worse. They were the biggest, fattest, ugliest insects she'd even seen—and she had lived in Florida! These happy bugs comfortably crawled within dark chocolate-like ridged folds that lined the sides of the tank. The sour-milk aroma from the hot sewage became thicker. Annette's stomach clenched. Her throat clamped shut. She looked away and tried to breath through her mouth. But she still saw those ecstatic bugs crawling with pleasure in the moist sludge.

"Color me gone," gagged Annette, dry heaving and scrambling down the ladder.

"How do you think Stinker's got his name?" casually said Koolner, enjoying her nausea. "Where is he?" He looked around the plant. "Stinker's, come to daddy!" No dog appeared. The old man endearingly said with a slight threat, "Stinker's, daddy loves you, come here." No dog appeared. Koolner took out the electrical device from the folds of his windbreaker. "He hates his thing. At first I didn't like using it, but now I kinda enjoy zapping him." Koolner pressed the button on the black box. A dog yelped. It came out from behind the water slide chutes and ran toward his master. Koolner closed the tank's opening. He descended the ladder. The dog cowered before him. Koolner sharply said to Annette, "Can your partner be trusted?"

"Yes."

"I know Joe," continued Koolner. "The guy is brilliant. He's a master at using people. Has she done anything to make you think she was telling Joe about—"

"She's telling him nothing. If she was, believe me I would know."

"Fine."

Annette looked down at the concrete walk and said, "I know this is none of my business, but—"

"Go ahead, you indulged me so I like you," Koolner cheerfully said, beaming.

"Why do you hate this place so much? I mean it must have been so beautiful back then, why wouldn't you just want to keep it that way? Why do you want to ruin it?"

Koolner lied, "I like to think young."

She had Malibu eyes. When the young Koolner looked within them, he was surrounded in turquoise. He was caught inside by the wave of her glance. Her gaze held him under, he didn't know where the surface or the bottom was. All Koolner saw was a blue sparkle. The gaze's turbulence squeezed his body inwards. He had no idea where he was and didn't even believe in himself. Just as a shark's organs are kept in place by the pressure of its ocean, the focus and discipline of Koolner's career drive was maintained by working out deals, writing press releases, and trying to make use of any scheme or a smile to get a buck. But when a shark is pulled out of its pressurized environment, all its organs collapse and can slide out of its mouth. That's what happened to Koolner when his mind left his fiscal world and his passion carried him up to her face into those Malibu eyes. His internal world fell out. He tortuously chewed on himself as he tumbled within the blue gaze. But unlike a shark, which has no nervous system so it feels no pain, Koolner had slight one, but it was his only one, and he tasted and felt a dried longing for this woman.

This perfect woman lacked only one quality: she didn't love him. But maybe she could, maybe...

Koolner dated her once. He spotted her at Malibu. He had just finished showing a beach house to an actor. Later that evening, she met Koolner at the restaurant for dinner. She seemed to like him. Her blonde hair, the thin and toned body, and those eyes. He instinctively knew the kind of wife she would be: healthy, sincere, nurturing, and active. He talked about his future and his goals. She left early, but said she'd be down at the beach the next day. Koolner went down to Malibu to see her. He wanted to tell her he didn't want to date her, he wanted to marry her. It was a September afternoon. He stood by his Lincoln. It was parked on a dirt shoulder along the Coast Highway. He wore a black suit and white shirt with tie, but he was thin and awkward. He looked at Malibu. There were six surfers out. The young Koolner felt no pull toward it. He scanned for her on the beach or in the water.

"My friend, can you give us a jump, my friend?" shouted the man from the back seat of a Mercury. "We had the radio on for awhile and the battery died."

Koolner approached the car. There was a naked couple inside.

"Just open the door," said Koolner.

"I can't, my friend," said the surfer. "It's all electric. Electric locks, electric windows. We can't get out."

A woman giggled.

The laughter seemed to twist a path between Koolner's lungs. She was with him. Koolner felt a part of himself sink and disappear into an area so deep he'd never be able to retrieve it. He was furious. Koolner stomped back to his car.

"Hey, how about that jump?"

Koolner slammed his car door, peeled out, and drove away. He knew the guy. He was Tommy Campion. He was a lifeguard who did some caretaker work at some of the Koolner family bungalows (not any more, thought Koolner.). Campion was a beach bum who surfed The Bu all summer. The guy was a loner. He didn't like people and he didn't like bosses. If she wanted a bum like Campion, fine. What prospects did any of these surfers have? Koolner had a successful real estate business, he was even doing press relations for some of the stars whom he sold houses on the other side of the pier. If she wanted to hang out with drunk bums who surfed and lived in a shed, fine. He'd prove her choice wrong. But it was more than that. Koolner knew Campion was everything he could never be. The man was muscular, had an uncritical zest, loved the ocean. He could act on his passions, and animated the sea with his skills. Well, Campion would have to leave the beach sometime and provide for himself or her one day. And Koolner would be waiting for him.

But the memory of her drew Koolner out like a rip current, and when he fought, it only made it worse, so all he could do was drift with it until it let him go, far away from his comfortable bed. Koolner did anything to avoid it, but even after he found someone and made love, he'd lay on his side and see her Malibu eyes rising up from the darkness, taking him out to sea again.

The entrance was concealed by wiry brown brush covering a cleft in a canyon of the nearby Santa Monica Mountains. It was dry, dusty, and hot. For thirty feet, Joe and Crispy uncomfortably wended through a narrow rocky crevice that lead to the cave. Their knees were scraped. They were sweating and cranky. Cool air came from the slightly illuminated entrance ahead. It calmed them. Joe entered first. The old drunk followed.

"Bitchen," said Crispy, standing up and looking around the cavern.

"Uh, welcome to the safety deposit box of Don Jose Bartolema's son, Tiburncio Tapai," grandly said Joe, gesturing about the cave. "He was a smuggler. Hid this stuff in here." Joe clicked his cheeks and tapped his sunglasses. "When it comes to greed, it pays to know your history."

The cave opened to a height of twenty feet. There was no lack of water or sunlight. A spring flowed from the base of a wall. Natural fissures allowed light throughout. The air was dry but not too cool. All the moisture seemed to be absorbed by the spring.

"Jez—"

"It was suppose to be my retirement fund," sadly said Joe.

All around the cavern there were intricately woven baskets, some with narrow bottoms and wide tops, others were circular or oval shaped with plain twining. Crispy saw steatite stone tools, sandstone flat-bottomed mortars and bowls, barbless stone hooks, remnants of sea grass nets, asphalton-sealed pottery, piles of shell necklaces, doughnut-shaped rocks, stone rings, pestles and balls, and gold jewelry. But what widened Crispy's eyes was a balsa surfboard designed by Simmons.

"Bitchen," he said, holding the surfboard, sliding his hands along its varnished rails. "God, he knew how to make a killer board. Man, narrowing the tail for speed and better turns, and broadening the nose. Bringing the rails up. Then throwing in a little rocker for looseness. Even an upturned nose so you didn't purl. The guy was ahead of his time. He was always talking about 'planing hulls.' His boards were fast. He had weather charts and knew when the swell would hit and where. We didn't know what swell direction meant back then. He put it together, though."

"It was my father's," said Joe. "It took me awhile to track down the owner. But I got the board back. Real cheap." He took the board from Crispy and gently laid it down, as if the object were a sleeping child he didn't want to awaken. "I'm going to take my Aloha Wave on this board."

"You really found a Malibu?" doubtfully asked Crispy.

"It's here," said Joe, unrolling the map out on the cool earthen floor, "Takes any swell, never gets too big, four to six foot."

"You know," said Johnson, pointing to the location on the map. "I always thought that place would work."

Joe lowered his sunglasses, raised his eyebrows, and smirked at his buddy.

Slick and Purpus watched a set of five waves perfectly peel from the outside point for a distance over five hundred yards to the pier, the only thing stopping the wave from continuing its perpetual reform was the lack of water. A swarm of fifteen imperfect shortboarders rapidly paddled out to the incoming set of waves. Their leash cords seemed to extend like wires from their shortboards to electric-clamps on their ankles. Slick thought the aggressive teenagers resembled robots powered by batteries within their boards. They all turned and took off on the same wave. The shortboarders vertically traveled up and down the hurtling shoulder. Their erratic surfing consisted of tight and snappy scissor-clipping turns at the bottom and the top. The three-finned boards gouged jagged openings into the waves. Foam billowed out from beneath their tails, as if the wave were a living creature, and the squiggling shortboarders were gutting out its puffy white organs and collapsing its shape.

"That's not surfing. That's vandalism," said Slick, snorting in disgust at the shortboarders. "Rip, tear. They don't seem to be riding the wave. They look like they're trying to kill it. Shortboarders. They've replaced the soul of style with an adrenaline rush. They think the rush is stoke. They're confused."

"You a purist?" asked Purpus, sitting in the sand beside his buddy.

"Where's the style?" decried Slick to the unknown. "Where's the grace?" His eyes narrowed in hostility. "See how ugly they look? Do they look like they're having fun? They just look angry. Every wave makes them more and more hostile. They're like aliens. I have no use for them. Their energy bores me beyond recognition. Look at'em. No matter how good they are, they all look the same. Years ago, when I'd come down here, I'd wake up in my car, up right on the cliff where Koolner's house is now, and from way up there I could watch everyone and without seeing their faces I could tell who everyone was by the way they rode. Now, they've all chosen to look the same. The board forces them to be that way." Slick spit in the sand and added, "I don't want the board to perform, *I* want to perform."

A shortboarder drove down to the bottom of the wave, snapped his board around, went vertically up the face, and smacked his board off the pitching lip. He flew into the air, grabbed his board by the side rail, turned it around so the nose pointed downward, and slid into the breaking foam and back into the shoulder. The other shortboarders hooted and howled.

"Look at that, they don't even want to ride the wave!" said Slick, shaking his head.

"It looked kinda neat to me," said Purpus, shrugging. "I mean if I was a kid, you know, I might like doing that."

A group of surfers in their thirties walked by. They were carrying longboards. They wore shirts that said "Malibu Longboard Union." They clearly recognized Slick.

"Hey brah, you going to go out and get some waves, brah?" said one of alleged adults to Slick.

"Yeah brah," added another split-ended blonde in the bunch, smiling.

"Let's surf together, get a nice sesh," chimed the third, doing a hang loose gesture with his hand by turning his three middle fingers into his palm and sticking out his thumb and pinkie.

"Fuck you," crisply snapped Slick, waving them away

The young men briefly broke their stride, but kept walking.

"Gez, Slick, you're just one giant ball of happy today, aren't you?" said Purpus. "What brought that on? They were just being friendly."

"Shit, all those guys that act so soulful on the beach, fuck them. I know them," said Slick, scowling, and spitting in the sand. "Nice guys on the beach, but just *add* water and they become complete dicks. They try to paddle around you and snake you every wave. They're full of shit, man. That's why I don't like those longboard kooks. They're a bunch of pyros. They sit in the bowl, see you coming down the line, and burn you anyway. They smile and do that to the people they know and work with. That's how they live their lives. Being two-faced. They think it's funny until someone does it to them. This place is just an extension of everything else. They act like the water is money." He watched the trio kneepaddle out. They come to me for validation. And they know if I say hello to them, they think I acknowledge them. No way. No validation from me, bro. They're the worst kind of kooks, because they don't think they're kooks." He picked up a kelp pod from the sand and popped its bulb. "I have more respect for a totally clueless person who is out there just trying to enjoy themselves, they're not trying to scam waves. They're just having fun. I let the clueless burn me any time." He paused, then looked straight at his cousin. "That's why I've always liked your style."

"At least they're on longboards," said Purpus.

"No matter what they say about longboards coming back, no way," said Slick, shaking his head. "It's sixties surfing in the nineties and nothing is going to change that."

"Don't hold anything back, tell me how you really feel," added Purpus, smiling.

"There's the best surfer in the whole place," said Slick, pointing to the shorebreak.

A six-year old boy rode his yellowed nine-foot board in the foam from a broken wave.

"'The best surfer is the one who has the most fun'—that's what Phil Edwards said," noted Slick, looking off.

They watched the boy paddle out.

"You ever regret not having a son, Slick?"

"Yes," Slick said quickly.

"Me too," said Purpus without hesitation

"Boy or girl?"

121

"I wouldn't care, as long as *he's* not a goofy foot," said Slick. They laughed.

"Hey Skip, what happened to the nose of your surfboard?" asked Slick examining the yellowed foam showing through the cracked fiberglass.

"Some moron ran me over out there," said Purpus, shaking his head. "He actually went out of his way to run me over."

"Welcome to the world of Surfer Joe."

"That was him?" said Purpus, more intrigued than angry.

"You missed the show," said Slick, squeezing the water from the ding. "Joe got into it with some shortboarders. You know, in the old days, Joe deserve to get beat on, but he never got into fights. He'd let it get to that point and then he'd back down." Slick laughed. "Actually it was kinda nice watching him get his clock cleaned."

"He's an asshole," said Purpus, looking down at the sand.

"Joe's a jerk," said Slick, putting the board down. "But, Joe is right. It was a better time to be alive. The surfing was better. The water was cleaner. You had a choice of whether you wanted to be out of work or not. Hey, it's definitely better than this." Slick made a sweeping gesture to the packed beach. His eyes narrowed. He winced. "Yesterday a punk called me a fucking troll."

"Huh."

"Yeah," said Slick, throwing a fist full of sand down.

Skip looked at the sullen Slick. For the first time Slick seemed a little haggard, the flesh on his face sagged a bit. He was beaten in a way. But he seemed noble to Skip. Maybe, Slick took surfing slights at Malibu a little too personally, but at least he followed his passion. Slick had his style. He made his own boards. He could build his own house and survive. Skip could do none of these things. And really, how many people could? How many were really willing to say what they felt, and stand there and force you to deal with them? Most would simply disassemble like bureaucrats, avoid the confrontation, and move on. But not Slick. You had to pass through him. That's a life, thought Skip, that's a life to be about.

"Oooooowha!" squealed the six-year old kid as a wave broke, driving the boy on the board straight down. He disappeared. The board went to shore. A brief second later he spurted up like a dolphin, eyes closed, shaking his whole body.

"It's the first drop of your wet dream kid," said Slick, smiling.

"It ruined me forever," said Purpus.

"No argument," added Slick.

Phrancky sat in the jacuzzi on Koolner's porch. She flicked back her blonde hair, reached over, picked up her glass, and took a sip of a Mai Tai. She glanced at her watch. It was safe to make the call. Annette was with Koolner at the treatment plant, probably conspiring to squeeze her out of the money, thought Phrancky, who didn't trust those two. That's why she was making this call. Phrancky picked up the portable receiver and dialed the pay phone number down at The Bu.

"Surfer Joe at you cervix," said the voice at the other end.

"We're suppose to whack you at Kahuna's," said Phrancky to Surfer Joe. "We're suppose to plant a note on you that will lead the cops to all the bodies."

"Nice tight little package," said Joe. "Why is Koolner letting me kill these guys so easily?"

"Like I could care, " said Phrancky. "The guy is sneaky. He's working on something, I don't know what it is, but he has these plans on his desk he gets rid of anytime I'm around. I don't trust that old fuck."

"How much is he paying to wipe me out?"

"Eighty thousand. It's suppose to be at his house tonight. When Annette...ummm, I mean, *you*, not Annette."

"I know what you mean."

"Well, when you and I come over. Of course, he won't expect to see you."

"Just remember to take the bullets out of the rifle," said Joe. "I'll take care of the rest."

"You don't have to remind me, I'm a professional. There won't be real bullets." She paused. "I'll do it, I'm not stupid."

"I never said you were," said Joe.

She hung up.

Surfer Joe put the receiver down, He leaned against the phone stall. The phone rang again. Joe picked up and said, "Uh, I thought I told you never to call me here, darling."

"We're still suppose to whack you when you get out of Kahuna's shop," said Annette.

"I'm going to be heading over there soon," said Joe, clicking his cheek. "Don't forget to switch rifles."

"Hey, I'll do it, I'm not stupid," defensively said Annette

"I never said you were," said Joe, hanging up.

Surfer Joe was pleased. He felt safe. If Annette decided to cross him and use a real gun, she would unknowingly be loading it with fake bullets put there by Phrancky; and, if Phrancky decided to cross him by using real bullets, she would be loading real bullets into a fake gun. Joe took this precaution for insurance, this way, if one of the women decided not to follow the program to make more money killing Joe—well, Joe was covered.

"Play the kooks against each other on their wave of greed," said Joe, doing a soul arch and wrapping his toes over the curb. "Styling."

Chapter
six

Stuffed in the foam

Slick sat at the concrete table in front of the El Acapulco Cantina, a Mexican take-out joint that was a five minute walk South of The Bu on the Coast Highway. The eatery was right across the street from Kahuna's Malibu Surf Shop. Slick's longboard was angled from the table and blocked part of the sidewalk. He wore faded swim trunks, sandals, and a paint-spattered sweatshirt. His uncombed hair resembled a haystack. The cantina's tacky thirty-foot adobe Mexican bandito stood behind him like a sentry. Slick powered down a bacon-and-egg burrito, and slurped a black coffee. He keenly checked out the sun-tanned women in throng bathing suits who were rollerblading and listening to music on earphones. Occasionally, a passing car honked and someone waved at him.

"Slick, you ought to quit surfing, then you could be a legend like me," shouted Kahuna. He slid two longboards into the back of a long trailer, which was attached to a pick-up truck. Kahuna wore painter's pants, a black shirt, and resin-spattered boots. He was in his fifties. More stout than stocky. His skin was pale as a foam blank. He had grayish-tinged black hair, a beard, and a black patch over his right eye. He was completely covered with foam dust. "How'z it?" he asked Slick.

"Head high—with assholes," answered Slick, throwing the

burrito wrapper into the trash. He picked up his board and jogged across the Coast Highway.

"Malibu. I haven't surfed Malibu since 1967," said Kahuna, scratching a fiberglass itch under his waistband.

"Yeah, come to think of it, everybody out there was asking where you've been."

"Leave your board in the truck," said Kahuna. "I want to show you a little project. Make you a business proposition."

They walked into the store. A cat meowed from underneath a spiral metal rack of Hawaiian shirts.

"I hate cats," clipped Slick. "No loyalty."

"That's Wayner," said Kahuna. "Hi, Wayner."

The orange-and-white cat rapidly pranced like Richard Dreyfuss past them. Wayner went behind the wetsuit rack along the rear of the store.

"Aren't you going to lock the door?" asked Slick.

"We'll only be a minute."

A phone van pulled up in from of the surf shop and parked behind Kahuna's truck. A white Mustang was parked catty-cornered across the highway. The two figures inside 1965 Ford had a clear view of the van's back doors.

Surfer Joe quietly entered Kahuna's surf shop. He listened. He heard voices. Joe walked to the back of the shop, peaked through an opening in the bamboo curtain and looked down a long hallway, which lead to the shaping room. Kahuna showed a longboard to Slick.

"The Beach Boys are going to introduce these boards," said Kahuna. "They agreed to paddle out on them and present trophies to the winner. A little promo."

Joe turned and walked away. He browsed about the surf shop. It was everything he hated. The place looked like a clothing department in a shopping mall chain store. Joe wove through the floor racks that held over-sized t-shirts, beach clothing, tie-dyed outfits, huge and baggy shorts, and string bikinis. Lining two walls, positioned sideways, were sixty brightly colored tri-fin shortboards. Their pointed noses and narrow round shapes resembled war shields. The ceiling had track lighting. In one corner, were changing rooms with small saloon doors in the middle. On either side of the cash register, were long glass cases stocked with sunglasses, sun screen, wax, and stickers. Behind the cases, was a pegboard wall with dangling leash cords. Above the leash display was a cartoon of Kahuna's eye-patched face, and below his head was the phrase: "Kahuna: Inventor of the leash: 1969."

"Kook cords," softly hissed out Joe, tapping his sunglasses.

Surfer Joe's Journal

The kook cord (known as the leash cord) is the main reason Kahuna must be tried as a surf-industry war criminal and strung up. He did it with blood money from foam dust.

Like all insidious devices, the kook cord is simple. An ankle strap with Velcro lining is wrapped around a surfer's ankle. The strap is connected to a hard but flexible, three-sixteenth-inch, urethane plastic cord. The cord is attached to a strap that ties to the deck of the surfboard by the tail. The length of the leash is usually the same length as the surfboard. In the late sixties, Kahuna experimented with the leash. He tried different types of cords. One of the cords was too elastic. Kahuna fell off his board and surfaced. The stretched-out leash made his board snap back too quickly, poking his right eye out. I love karma.

Before the kook cord, surfers need to learn wave judgment and positioning. Surfers were required to hang onto their boards, and, if they couldn't, they had to possess the ability to swim long distances to retrieve them. This reality or the possibility of drowning, and being hit by your board, or both, intimidated kooks from taking up surfing. Kooks were never good enough to hang onto their boards, which meant other surfers would get hit by loose boards. True, without a leash, the board would go to the beach, and the kook was out of everybody's way for twenty minutes. Sometimes a kook was so exhausted from the swim, he left or gave up surfing. Kooks were filtered out by their own limitations. But, with the leash, any kook could just paddle out, lose his board, swim a few feet over to it, and be back out in the lineup in just a few minutes.

Kahuna watered down the quality of surfers in the ocean.

The concrete foam blank mold looked like an open coffin in the small empty room. It stood against the wall by a door that led to Kahuna's shaping room. The mold was a twelve-foot long by three-foot wide square block. Its concrete lid was held up by two chains that ran through hooks on its top and up through a pulley system suspended from the ceiling. It rested on three-foot high legs.

"This is one of the molds from Grubby's shop?" asked Slick.

"Yeah," said Kahuna. "I'm coming out with a classic version of the Malibu Pig board I made in the fifties. Narrow nose, wide hips."

"Kinda like you."

"Hey, a lot of guys are willing to pay big bucks for classic boards as wallhangers," said Kahuna. "I can sell these sticks for fifteen hundred dollars. I make them with heavy glass, dense blanks, glassed-on wooden fins. You know, take the kook money."

Slick smelled resin; it irritated his nose and made his eyes water. He liked it. They went to the shaping room door. It had a poster of a model in a bikini.

"My girlfriend," said Kahuna, pointing to the photo.

"She broke up with me for cheating on her," said Slick.

"Yeah, right," snorted Kahuna.

The shaping room's shelves were filled with numerous items: rolls of fiberglass woven fabric, sandpaper, wax paper, adhesive tape and several sandwich bags filled with q-cell powder. Any possible opening on the black walls was plastered with photographs of models from swimsuit catalogues sent to the shop. There were pegboards with tools on hooks—grinders, files, etc. On the floor, beside a compressor, was a bunch of curved pasteboard template strips. And near the pile, a small work bench was stacked with fiberglass cloth strips, a gauze breathing mask, sander and polishing pads, razor blades, scissors, calipers, a paint-spattered portable radio, and four empty beer cans. There were waist-high florescent lights on opposite walls. Two three-foot t-shaped support posts stood in a corner. Everything was coated with a fine white powder.

"Here's the wave of the future," said Kahuna, holding up a longboard with a pointed nose, hard rails, a curved rocker, three-fins, and a drawn down tail. It was thin and narrow. The board was bright orange and painted with flames.

"Whoa," said Slick, picking up the board, surprised by its lightness. "What is this, ten?"

"Twelve pounds. And it's nine-six."

"It's just a long shortboard, what's the big deal?" impassively said Slick, shrugging.

"Trust sales, the modern longboard is going to be the next big thing," said Kahuna, rubbing his unshaven face. "The Beach Boys are going to introduce these boards. They agreed to paddle out on them and present the trophies to the winner of the contest. A little promo."

"You were always good at that," said Slick. "You are always good at that."

"You missed the first wave, Slick," said Kahuna. He paused. "Good chance to pick up some cake. Get yourself a retirement nut together." He paused. "All those older guys respect you. You can get a second chance—"

"Why does everyone think I want a second chance?"

Kahuna's eyes' glimmered and he said, "Sure you do. You got burned by Joe."

"Joe was out there today, getting happy."

"Yeah, right," huffed Kahuna, his leathery skin deeply crinkling. "Surfer Joe can never come back here. There are too many guys who remember him."

"Serious," said Slick. Kahuna's face went flat, as if it were turned off. "Did you hear about Buzzy?" asked Slick.

Kahuna was engrossed in a distant memory. He grunted to himself, "Koolner."

"Yeah, Koolner told me Joe's killing everyone in 'The Gidget' movie," said Slick.

"You're telling me Joe's stuffing The Crew because of a fucking movie?" asked Kahuna, clearly jarred. "Koolner never told me this."

"I'm surprised, after all, you guys go *way* back," quipped Slick, smirking.

"Hey, fuck you Slick!" said Kahuna, who caught the subtle implication. "I know what you mean by that. Well, I paid for my share. I worked for it. I earned my freedom."

"How much did it cost?" asked Slick, turning to leave the shaping room. He walked down the hallway and out through the bamboo curtains that lead to the front of the surf shop.

"I guess getting through the sixties selling dope was such a saintly thing for you to do." said Kahuna, following Slick out the door to the sidewalk.

"I didn't know *killing* somebody was such a saintly thing to do either," said Slick, picking his board from the trailer. "I guess that's why we go to different churches." He walked away.

"Go back to your Malibu, beach bum," yelled Kahuna, standing outside the surf shop. "Go rule your fucking kingdom and see who comes to help you."

Slick walked north to the beach, and stood on the sidewalk by the phone stall. The phone rang.

"Hello," said Slick, answering it.

"Yeah, I was calling for a surf check, is there a swell?"

"Where you calling from?"

"The San Fernando Valley."

"It's flat," said Slick, hanging up.

Slick looked at The Bu. It was more crowded and the waves were just peeling in. Slick was definitely in a foul enough mood to deal with the mob. He wanted to get into it with someone. If Malibu was the last refuge for a kook, where they could steal, use brute strength, be rude, and inconsiderate, and still get what they want. So, Slick reasoned, if Malibu was the last place to be wrong, it was also the last place where he could be right, where he could be his own hero, where a kook could really be put in their proper category. Malibu. The only place left where Slick could rule.

Kahuna closed the door, locked it, and went to the back of the shop. When he parted the bamboo curtains, hangers clanged on the rack to his right. He whirled with fists up. His eye darting.

An orange-and-white cat emerged from behind a row of wetsuits.

"I'm getting paranoid," said Kahuna to himself, laughing.

His patched eye didn't see the figure springing toward him.

Joe slipped a looped leash over Kahuna's head, tightening the cord around his neck. He dragged Kahuna on his back across the floor. They went through the curtain and down the hallway toward the shaping room.

"Oooooougggggha," said Kahuna.

"Let's go surfing," whispered Joe, pulling his prey into the empty room. "Nice invention your leash. It's going to bring you right back to your board."

Kahuna flailed his arms around, trying to pull the cord off his throat. Joe released the cord. Kahuna collapsed, gasping. Joe kicked Kahuna in the groin, rolled him over on his stomach, tightly tied his arms together with one leash cord, and used another leash as a gag.

"Are you happy you made all your money in foam?" vehemently asked Joe. "Foam, where the kooks surf. Foam."

"Joeeah," said Kahuna, chewing into the leash cord.

"First I have to see something," said Joe, reaching down and pulling Kahuna's eye patch back. "Ooooooh, you really did lose that eye to a leash cord. I thought it was just a marketing ploy." Joe blew into the hollow muscled-sealed socket. He sullenly said, "I thought it would make a sound." He let the eye patch go. It snapped back on its thin elastic band. Kahuna twinged as it stung him. Joe pulled the patch back and repeated the process three or four times. He stopped. Joe browsed around the shaping room. "Uh, a kitchen of the past," lovingly said Joe, tilting his head. "It brings back memories, most of them frequent and very unpleasant." Joe opened the closet. "Uh, styrene, acetone, laminated or sanding resin. Hmmmm. I'll probably go with the sanding resin."

"Neeeaaah," said the man on the floor.

"Kahuna, I want to show you my recipe for revenge. It's called 'Malibu Pig Surprise'."

"Aaaaarha," said Kahuna, saliva coating the leash in his mouth.

"First you need a Malibu pig," said Joe, lifting Kahuna and dropping the squirming man into the open concrete mold. Joe tapped his sunglasses. "I forgot to turn on the oven." He hit the switch on the mold.

Youa," burbled Kahuna.

Joe ignored the man and went into the side room, returning with a few small barrels of chemicals, and an electric mixer. He filled one barrel with a white liquid, added the expanding catalyst, and mixed them. The chemicals expanded into a fizzing white foam that rose up and overflowed the bucket's lip to the floor.

"Now, we must add several parts of foam and mix various chemical additives for extra body." said Joe pouring the mixture onto Kahuna. "A little chant will help to get the mixture to reach its ideal state: From foam dust you were born and from foam dust you will return, oh great spirit."

"Arraaallaugha," said Kahuna, his mouth filling with the glop as he thrashed and kicked, spraying out flecks of foam.

"Now that we have achieved all the proper prerequisites," cheerfully said Joe, releasing the chains that held the mold open. "You're ready to cook your Malibu... Pig..."

"Aaaaaaha!" Kahuna screamed as the lid slammed down.

"Surprise'!" said Joe, clamping the top down. "And, it serves *one* right."

"He's been in there for three hours," glumly said Phrancky, taking a sip of diet soda. The rifle between her legs pointing downward by the car's brake.

"What's the matter?" asked Annette, trying to move her bulky butt about in the passenger seat. "Why the fuck did you get such a small car?"

"Because it's cool."

"Well, it doesn't *feel* cool," grunted Annette, shifting about. "You could of at least parked behind the jerk so we wouldn't have to turn around."

"I just hope this piece of shit Carcano works," said Phrancky, examining the weapon. She hefted the rifle. She furrowed her brow. "This feels different."

"Looks the same to me," said Annette, shrugging.

Phrancky loaded real bullets into the weapon. The Gidget offered her more money than Joe, but that also included getting rid of Koolner too. It didn't matter who died to Phrancky, as long as she got the most bang for the buck. Now, Annette was out of the loop. Phrancky suspected Annette and Koolner were going to get rid of her. Well, that wasn't going to happen.

"He's coming out of the shop," eagerly said Annette. "It's crunch time"

Joe shielded himself with an orange longboard. He went into the rear of his van and closed the doors behind him.

"Shit, I couldn't get a clear shot," said Phrancky, lowering the rifle. "He must suspect something."

"Don't look at me."

Phrancky suspiciously clipped, "There was no reason for me to do that—until now."

"He'll come out."

The doors of the van flew open. Joe held a M-79.

"Jesus!" said Annette. "He wasn't suppose to—

Phrancky sighted the rifle and pulled the trigger. Nothing

happened, just a flat click.

"I rigged the gun," sighed Annette, realizing Joe set them up. Phrancky glared at her. Annette rolled her eyes and added in a snippy tone, "I don't even want to talk about it."

A soft pneumatic-like thoooomp came from the M-79. A blur streaked from its muzzle toward the Mustang. The car exploded. Its frame rocked off the street. Flaming chunks spiraled into the air. The car laid sideways. Both women became living swirls of flames. They screamed horrifically.

Joe looked up from the M-79, calmly viewed their agony, and said, "Uh, that's the way they would have wanted to go."

Slick surfed across a wave, carrying a shortboard under his arm. He laid it sideways in the tumbling white water behind him. The foam took the shortboard to shore, and smashed it up on the softball-sized rocks. Just before the wave dumped on the beach, Slick deftly kicked out. He slid off his board, stood up to his knees in the water, tucked his stick under his right armpit and walked to shore.

"Hey troll!" screamed a twenty-year old kid.

Troll. There was that word again. The sound of it made Slick's insides buckle and bind. Slick stopped. He stood in the wet sand. The waves lapping his ankles.

"Next time don't snake me cheesedick," said Slick, not even turning toward the guy. Instinctively, he knew the kid was going to throw a punch at his head. Slick turned around with his board angled to block the blow. A fist banged on the deck. Slick heard the minute cracking sound of finger bones.

"Fuck!" screamed the punk.

Slick lowered his board. The buzzcut punk stared through his war-paint sunscreen at his broken hand. It was swelling.

"Jez, that looks like it really hurts," said Slick, grinning.

"Troll—"

Slick shoved the guy into the sand, stood over him and shouted, "Don't ever call me a troll, you gyro butt-wiggling kook!"

"I'm charging you with assault," whimpered the buzzcut, looking for a lifeguard.

"You came at me, Booger Ring," said Slick, pointing his

finger at the youth's jeweled nostrils. "You wanna file an assault charge?" He shoved the kid. "I'll make sure you're really assaulted. But go ahead, call the lifeguard over, I taught him how to surf. See who's side he's on?" Slick narrowed his eyes. "And I want to tell you something else, cheesedick, you don't even know who I am do you? I suggest you find out."

The kid glared, walked away, and shouted. "Fucking troll!"

Slick put down his board, tackled Booger Ring, picked him up, and stuffed him into a garbage barrel.

"Making friends, Slick?" asked Crispy, who started to chuckle and wound up hacking.

"Just trying to pack my trash," said Slick, walking away from the can and over to his friends.

Crispy had on the same clothes from the day before. He showed a little wear from last night's binge. His face was a little puffed, scraped, and purplish. He drank from a bottle in a paper bag. A tanned Purpus sat on a blanket, his legs up and his elbows rested on his knees.

"I thought you weren't going to go surfing," said Purpus.

"It wasn't what I call surfing," said Slick, putting down his board.

The kid rocked the drum, it tipped over on the sand. He tried to squirmed out with the garbage.

A huge explosion like a giant closeout rolled down the Coast Highway. They saw a coil of deep black smoke near the surf shop.

"Kahuna," slowly said Slick.

They picked up their boards and ran to the fire.

"The Big One," jubilantly shouted Crispy, chuckling and staggering behind them.

The twisted, blackened frame of the 1966 Mustang convertible was in flames, smelling of burnt meat and melted rubber. The heat kept the crowd ten feet back from the mangled wreckage. Shattered glass was everywhere. The hood was ripped apart. The car's body was riddled with hundreds of small holes. Two blackened skeletons were tangled in the springs of the melted bucket seats. The corpses had their hands around each other's necks.

"What a waste," said Purpus.

"Yeah, a 1966 Mustang, what a classic," sadly said Slick, shaking his head.

Purpus laughed.

They heard a siren in the distance. Cars were backing up in both directions. Horns honked.

"The Big One is coming!" said Crispy like a preacher.

"It's just a car, Crispy, lighten up," said Slick, exasperated. "A fucking car."

"I'm sorry," muttered Crispy, looking across the block at the darkened surf shop. "Hey, shouldn't Kahuna's shop be open? It's past one."

"A sign on the door says "'Gone surfing,'" said Purpus

"He hasn't gone surfing in twenty years," said Slick.

The trio walked across the palm-branch strewn highway to Kahuna's. The shop's windows had four-foot long spider-leg cracks. Slick tried the door; it was unlocked. He raced to the shaping room, followed by Crispy and Purpus. Slick reached the shaping room first. The room reeked with resin and acetone.

A human longboard laid across two wooden saw horses in the center of the room. Kahuna was embedded within a ten-foot foam blank and coated with a clear shroud of hardened fiberglass. His face was burnt red and contorted. His lone eye bulged outside the socket like an overcooked hard-boiled egg. A ceramic pink snout was on his nose.

"Kahuna," said Slick.

"Yeah, it looks like one of his shapes," observed Crispy, smiling. "The Malibu Pig."

Joe sat on the floor of his van. He used a razor to cut a one-inch wedge from the nose of the modern longboard. His long canary yellow fingernails peeled back the excess fiberglass. Joe sanded down the jagged foam in the triangular opening, and placed tape across its bottom and hooked the tape up along its side. He gingerly filled the nose of the longboard with a compound resembling a whitish salt, but it wasn't as granular as salt, it was more buffed out. This was lead azite, a very impact-sensitive explosive. In fact, it was so sensitive, the azite powder had to be cut with other powders so the explosive's crystals wouldn't touch and detonate. It was powerful too, just one teaspoon could blow the head off a shovel. Joe put four heaping tablespoons in a small plastic container filled with q-cell mixture. He stirred it with a tongue depressor stick until catalyst made the white liquid thicker and heated it up. He poured the powerful syrupy batch into a three-inch triangular wedge cut into the nose of a modern longboard. The white mixture filled in the taped-off gap and hardened into a deadly warhead ding. Joe would have to wax up and personally deliver these boards to the Beach Boys, otherwise, some kook might drop the board, and blow up lesser victims.

"I might be able to kill the Beach Boys too," said Joe, cutting another wedge into the second modern longboard. He looked upward and added, "There is a God, and He doesn't like kooks."

Slick sat on the beach and appreciated the orange-yolk like sunset cracking on the edge of The Bu's horizon. Its colors spread across the glassy sheet of water and gave the surface an oily coppery look. Slick ate a fast-food burger and fries. He wore slightly ripped and faded jeans and a paint-spattered sweatshirt. A small cooler was by his sandaled feet. A seagull landed near him. Slick threw it a french fry. The bird gobbled it up.

"Ooooooowh," hooted a surfer.

Slick looked at one of the waves. Four people were on it. Surprisingly, Purpus was right in the curl, the others were ahead of him yelling at each other on the shoulder. At the end of his ride, Purpus jumped off his board and let it go. The board went forward in the foam, until it fully extended the ten-foot leash cord tethered to Purpus' ankle. He stood up to his knees in the shallow water, picked up the board, and nimbly stepped between some rocks until he reached the beach.

"When you finish on a wave, Skip, kick out before the wave closes," said Slick, looking hard into Purpus. He emphatically added, "The end of your ride is the last thing everyone sees."

"Huh?" said Purpus, who was wet, sunburnt, and out of it from his stoke.

"There's still a lot of kook in you I have to hammer out," said Slick, snorting. "Having a day job has nearly killed you."

"Yes sir," said Purpus, putting his board face down in the sand. He noticed the cooler. "Is there beer in there?"

"Oh no, there's no beer in there," said Slick, opening the lid and grabbing two beers. "They're not cheap, a million bucks."

"I'll get you back," said Purpus, removing the Velcro leash strap. He took a beer, which was so cold the metal can made his hand hurt. He gulped down two deep swallows. His head throbbed and his throat evenly burned with a delightful ache. He looked off at The Bu. "God, Calirfornia sucks. I wish I was In Newerk."

Slick smiled and peered at Skip. Water dripped from Purpus' matted hair and down his body. The guy was really stoked. Slick realized it'd been a long time since he felt that way. Slick came out of the water feeling like he survived an engagement with the enemy. Slick studied his stoked cousin, he had to admit, Slick had a lesson to learn from this New Jersey kook who liked the Beach Boys and just wanted to surf.

They slurped down the cold beers and enjoyed the salt breeze. The incoming coolness deadened the slight heat in the air. The ocean hissed. A distant seal oooar-ed. The evening was taming down the day. It was less hectic. The beach was nearly empty. There were only thirty people out in the ocean. The change in light made the white sand resemble brown sugar.

"This is when I usually go out," said Slick. "It's so peaceful."

A bullhorn-amplified voice blared: "All right, guys, we want scaffolding there, the judge's stand here,"

Slick and Purpus turned. They saw a crew of about twenty men. They wore white t-shirts, long madras pants, and neon-lime sneakers. Some with a higher rank wore orange baseball hats and windbreakers that said "The Gidget Invitational."

"Setting up for tomorrow's goddamn contest," plaintively sighed Slick, scowling. "Figures, anytime this place gets close to a perfect moment some kook finds a way to ruin it." He flicked another fry to a small seagull. "Some of us only get scraps left by others." A larger bird cawed, raised its wings, drove away the smaller bird and greedily ate the abandoned fry.

"It's a cold world," said Purpus, nodding.

Slick angrily threw sand at the big bird and said, "Get the fuck out of here! Big seagull, I don't like you. I am God here. And you, will not eat my fries." The bird flew off. The smaller seagull returned. Slick threw the bird a fry. "Here you go, buddy."

"Don't you think we should have gone to the cops?" asked Purpus.

"Fuck no," said Slick. "Let that Malibu mafia kill each other, they deserve each other."

"I mean do you think Joe *really* killed that guy?"

137

"I'm going to give you a piece of advice: 'Don't fight over somebody else's wave.'"

"Not my wave?" said Skip, confused.

"Look, it's just not your wave, let it go," said Slick, sucking in his lips and shaking his head. "Skip, let's say you're paddling to get into a wave, some burn artist is paddling out, spins his board around, and does a burn job by taking off in front of you, stuffing you in the foam and taking your wave. Okay, it's a little later, you're paddling back out and you see the burn artist paddling for another wave. It's payback time. Now, you're in the position to give him what he gave you. You spin around, take off in front of him, and stuff the burn artist. That's payback. But, someone else watching from the shore only sees that you burned the guy, they didn't see the wave before it." Slick spit. "You have to know the history behind the wave."

"And I don't know what Kahuna did to Joe before Surfer Joe did what he did to Kahuna."

"Correcto-mundo," replied Slick. "It's not your wave, it never will be."

"Hey, we're talking about a murder, not a wave," said Skip, scoffing. "But the cops will find him."

"No way, Cops are kooks," said Slick, shrugging.

"They got him once," said Skip, smirking.

Slick looked at the horizon and said, "Bitchen sunset."

"You ever ride Sunset?" asked Purpus, toweling off. "In Hawaii?"

"Is that where it is?" mockingly asked Slick. "Man we'd ride it with four people out. The rights just fired. It'd jack up and just freight train out. You have to have a real sack on you to ride that place. It was a bomber. The left is a death wish."

"The left?"

"You don't go left at Sunset. Real hairy. It'd suck up even faster on a reef and just rise up over your head and dump you right down into the bottom. But, if you make it. It was something to make. Most didn't." He smiled and raised his eyebrows. "Everyone has to go left at Sunset just once. "

"On our honeymoon, I wanted to go Hawaii, but my ex wanted to see go to Jamaica."

"Fuck," said Slick. "That should have told you right there."

"When we got married she said she loved ocean."

"You mean *before* you got married," corrected Slick.

"Yeah, before," said Purpus, nodding.

"There were a lot of things 'before' in mine too," said Slick, digging his feet into the sand.

Skip Purpus neutrally sat in his office cubicle. A small radio on the shelf near the computer played an oldies station. It was six in the evening, but Skip was in no hurry to get home. He rarely was. He looked down at his overhanging gut, grabbed it with his hands, and angrily squeezed. He was six-foot three-inches, weighed two-hundred and thirty pounds, and was thirty-seven years old. Thirty seven. And for fifteen of those years, he worked at this computer firm, writing press releases, newsletters, policies, etc. Fifteen years. Yeah. That's why he rated a corner cubicle with windows. It was an office he probably wouldn't occupy by next year. His firm, Trindex, was in the process of being bought out by another company. The new boys would do their housecleaning. They'd bring in their buddies, take the areas they wanted, and squeeze out any long-term employees. The present Vichy management was saying this wasn't going to happen, but at the same time, they were rewarding themselves with golden parachutes for driving the company into the ground, and leaving everyone else on board to crash. There wasn't a safety net for Skip to land in. Sure, he had a house in Freehold, New Jersey. But he foolishly bought high in the go-go Reagan eighties, and in the nineties Skip couldn't sell it without a $60,000 loss. Great, he thought, a house use to be a step up, now it was a stagger step back. And he didn't even want the house to begin with. His wife wanted the place. She wanted children too, but that was before they got married. Instead, she decided to continue her education. Skip supported her while she achieved her Ph.D. in nutrition, but after she received her degree, she didn't want to get a job, she wanted to take even more courses, and possibly teach part-time at a university. Her life was turning out just great. But, what was Skip getting? With increasing property taxes, state taxes, federal taxes, he worked until June to pay for everyone else's freight. It seemed to Skip that everyone was making out but him. If you were a drunk, poor or had a drug problem, you could receive food stamps, low-cost drugs, welfare, free education, counseling, low-interest loans, and housing. But there weren't low-interest loans for being a nice guy who worked hard. There was no help for a professional who was overeducated, unionless, without a practical trade. All Skip had was his ability to be professional with a sense of humor. Two qualities the world perceived as weaknesses that showed a lack of confidence. He looked at his life and felt he was out of the equation. What did he have to draw on within himself? It was *his* fault. He depended on others to provide for him. Skip let this corporate training lull, numb, and remove his territorial growl. There must be an escape valve...

The radio played the Beach Boys' tune "I Just Wasn't Made For These Times":

> I keep looking for a place to go where I can speak my mind
> And I've been trying hard to find the people I won't leave behind
> They say I got brains but they ain't doing me no good, I wish they could
> I guess I just wasn't made for these times.

The Beach Boys oohs and aaahs and vocals made the inside of Skip's skin vibrate. When he was a teenager, he listened to the Beach Boys with his buddies. They'd talk about learning to surf but never do anything about it. Purpus was afraid to try it. He wasn't built like a surfer. He was skinny, uncoordinated, and he couldn't swim well. But surfing haunted him. Maybe, thought Skip, if he was a surfer in his youth he wouldn't be sitting in this office. Who would he have become? He wanted a chance to relive that moment. Maybe, that's why he still had Slick's longboard in the rafters of the garage. Getting rid of it, would be like the final surrender. At first, his fiancé thought the longboard was neat. Now, his wife didn't understand why Purpus kept something he'd never use. But, he *could* use it. He was stronger, he wasn't skinny (actually he was too heavy, but he could lose the weight). He wasn't a good swimmer, but now, boards had leash cords. Sure, he didn't have trade skills, but he did have management options: stock options. Over the years, Skip wisely purchased and kept company stock. With the takeover, his stock was worth $275,000, and the money he vested into his retirement plan was a healthy chunk too. Why stay married? No kids, no love. Purpus could absorb the loss on the house. Hell, his wife could keep it. And he did have a freebie coming: Skip was entitled to a three-month paid sabbatical. What was to stop him from taking Slick's signature board down from the garage rafters and learning to surf? Nothing really. And maybe, he could even try writing about what he loved: surfing.

The song continued:

> Every time I get the inspiration to go change things around
> No one wants to help me look for places where they might be found
> Where can I turn when my fair weather friends cop out, what's it all about?
> I guess I just wasn't made for these times.

Skip listened to the Beach Boys song. His eyes brimmed and became a little glassy. It was as if all of the consequences of Skip's life had shifted the same way sand from a beach is arranged into a clean sand bar that creates a point. Now, Skip was definitely at the peak of a new break. He felt a second wave rising up underneath him. He was being given another chance. Purpus could go for it, or back down. If he decided to go for it, Skip had no idea where the calling would take him. He could end up a failure, broke, no medical plan, and stuck in a dead-end job. But that promising shoulder beckoned to him again. Where would this ride lead to? What qualities would it unearth in him that he buried and never tapped? Skip could play it safe and realistic and back down. He could let this opportunity pass, after all it was probably some panic phase: a guy wanting to relive his youth. That's what his brain told him, but he didn't want to listen to his brain, he wanted to follow his heart. Why not take off? Did he have anything worth keeping? Sure, he had medical benefits, but the reason he needed them was his company was making him sick. Really, what did he want to keep? Nothing. All he had to angle for was the promising rise of a green shoulder.

Skip went for it.

"They say it takes two to make a bad marriage," said Purpus, looking off at the orange band of sunset along the horizon. "But if you're not the one who changes, and that's why the person supposedly loved you, then how can it be your fault?" said Purpus, gulping down the beer. He thumped his chest and belched.

"So, what really put the bug in your head?" asked Slick.

"One day I was playing golf—"

"Golf?" said Slick, amused. "Golf: the *last* sport."

"Well, one of my Sunday-golf partners didn't show up for our foursome. He just left his fat wife and cut out. And I said, 'He just did what every guy at this club would do if they had the guts.'" He paused. "I realized I was talking about me, and I got scared."

Slick stuffed his half-eaten burger and fries into a bag, crumbled it, and threw it into a nearby garbage barrel. "Two points."

The two surfers watched the sun disappear. The orange afterburst reflected on the domed sky, which turned a deep blue fringed with darkness. They put their empty beer cans in the cooler and walked away.

"I kinda went left," said Purpus, shivering a little. He got up and grabbed his longboard.

"Well, you can't find an answer if you know what it is," said Slick, looking at the horizon.

"Bitchen sunset."

"It's behind us."

"You ever go left at Sunset?" asked Skip.

"Yeah, I got down in the tube. It was too fast. I got fucking blasted," said Slick, adding with the accomplished firmness of the redeemed. "But, I got the vision."

"Yeah," said Purpus, recalling his first sight of a rising shoulder, where he hoped to find a style.

The two surfers crossed the Coast Highway.

The smaller seagull pounced upon Slick's bag in the garbage can. The big gull returned, drove away the smaller bird, and devoured all the remains.

She waited for Koolner to pick up the phone.

"Surfer Joe is dead," said a woman in Phrancky's voice.

"Great," said Koolner at the other end. "I heard the explosion! What happened?"

"He had some explosives in the van."

"Fine."

"And Gidg—"

"She's gone, but it'll be a while before they figure out who she is."

"Payday, come around tonight," said Koolner, hanging up.

The Gidget held the phone and looked at Joe. He stood beside her at the Malibu phone stall. She hung up.

"Did I do good, Joey?" she simpered and pecked Joe's cheek with a kiss.

"Yes, you did good," he softly whispered.

Joe reached into his poncho pocket, took a red marker, and circled the last figure in The Pit Crew.

Chapter seven

Caught Inside

Surfer Joe stalked along the widow's walk of Koolner's mansion. In his left hand, Joe held an air-holed cardboard carrying case. He gently slid the glass door open. Joe heard AC-DC's "It's a Long Way to the Top." He peered down the hallway into the living room. The old man was dressed in a red satin bathrobe and bunny slippers, dancing wildly to the music. Koolner's back was to him. Joe entered the room and turned the stereo off.

"Your money is on the desk," cheerfully said Koolner, turning around. His face blanched at the sight of Joe in the leather hat, sunglasses, poncho, swimsuit, and sandals.

"Let's go surfing, my friend," said Joe, and from his poncho's pouch, he withdrew a nine-millimeter pistol.

"Stinkers!" commanded Koolner. "Protect."

The growling dog bounded out, eyes misfocused with rage. It drooled.

Joe carefully kept the gun on Koolner. Then, Joe dropped the box. Out popped the cat from Kahuna's shop. The stunned calico saw the dog. Stinkers saw Wayner. The cat hissed, raised his fur, and ran out the open porch door. Stinkers barked and chased it.

"Stinkers!" helplessly shrieked Koolner.

"Smart dog," said Joe, quickly closing the door.

"You're a little smarter," said Koolner in a snit.

"You know, you have too much, uh, self-possession," said Joe. "I think it's time to lose that." Joe, fired the gun, blowing apart a section of the parquet flooring under the old man's feet.

"Okay, okay, okay," rapidly said Koolner, his heavily veined hands trembling.

Joe smiled, "You know, I'm enjoying this more than I thought I would."

Stinkers slammed into the sliding glass door. He tried to smash it. Joe fired at the animal. Pulverized glass fragments spread everywhere like frozen snow crystals.

"Stay," said Joe. The dog didn't move. "Good dog."

"There's money, eighty thousand in small bills, right there on the desk," said Koolner. "Why don't you just take it and leave?"

"Oh, I'll take it, but I'll stay," said Joe, clicking his cheek. He put the money down and picked up the rolled blueprint. "What's this?" He opened the plans. It took a moment for him to grasp what he found. Koolner's eyes widened in fear. Joe's narrowed in hate.

"Let me explain," blubbered Koolner.

"Don't try to stall me," said Joe. "Your buddies aren't coming tonight. They're Mustang flambe." Koolner blinked. "They're all dead." He showed his gap-toothed grin. "It's time to get happy."

"Aieeeeeee!" screamed Koolner, sprinting for the door.

"You're mine," said Joe, lunging and tackling the old man. They slid across the floor. Joe's necklace snapped; teeth rattled.

"What do you care?" begged Koolner, clawing at Joe.

"Stay,' said Joe, smashing Koolner in the side of the head with a pistol. The old man crumpled into stillness. "Good Koolner."

Surfer Joe unzipped the inside pocket of his poncho and took out a video-cassette, along with numerous jacks, a fuse, receiver, and a timing device. He went outside and returned with several PETN datasheets. He rolled back a huge oriental rug, put down the sheets on the floor like tiles. By simply laying these sheets in the middle of the house, he significantly increased the explosion's shock waves, guaranteeing total annihilation of Koolner's estate. Joe wanted to eliminate any possibility Koolner's house would avoid destruction. All Joe had to do was connect an automatic timer to the VCR and TV, as well as install a special timer under the deck. It was a unique twist he had in store for *her*.

Joe poured himself a glass of wine. He swirled it, sharply sniffed the bouquet, and nodded appreciatively. He took the glass to the VCR, sat among the wires, and started working.

"I'm getting this place truly dialed," Joe whispered, clicking his cheek and adjusting his sunglasses.

Surfer Joe sat at the sixteenth century desk and studied the blueprint to Koolner's masterpiece. He marveled at the ingenuity of the old man's vindictiveness. The engineering plans were for a one-thousand foot, L-shaped jetty, which Koolner planned to position near the Malibu Creek rivermouth. This rock jetty would prevent the Winter storms from redistributing sand to taper the cobblestone reefs into slopes that perfectly picked up the South Swells. Without the sand, the ocean bottom's contour would be jagged and uneven, and produce sloppy and choppy surf that would section or break simultaneously without a shoulder. The pulse of a perfectly peeling wave with the moving peak would be gone forever. Malibu would be dead.

"Ooooh," groaned Koolner, moving in an awkward paddle across the floor, scattering seal teeth.

"Look what washed up," said Joe, standing over him. "By the way, how do you like your new charm bracelet?"

"My what?" said Koolner. He suddenly felt a jolt. "Ooooooh."

Stinker's electric-shock collar was on the old man's neck.

"I modified it a little," said Joe, rolling up the plans.

"Joe—"

"Quiet!" said Joe, hitting the button on the black box.

"Oooooh," moaned Koolner.

"You want to destroy Malibu to build a yacht harbors. A floating trailer park!" said Joe, with an edgy glint in his eyes.

"What's Malibu to you anyway?" defiantly asked Koolner, wincing as he lightly touched his red-syrup like cut. "You left it."

"This jetty. Building this jetty is why you were letting me take out the Pit Crew," said Joe, thwapping the rolled-up plans across the wound on the old man's head.

"They would have never gone along with it," blubbered Koolner. "They would have turned on me."

"You already fucking ruined Malibu. Why do you want to destroy it?" He paused. "You don't surf."

"Oh, because I don't *surf*, I should leave it alone to the surfers," venomously spat Koolner. "All you surfers think you're so free, so independent. You're living and I'm not. You're the dead ones." Koolner laughed. "If that sewage keeps going out into the water, who do you think is going to fight to protect a dead sea? Why protect it? Why not build something? Boats create tax and property revenues, harbors create businesses. What money does surfing bring in? Parking tickets? Deposit bottles? Who is going to listen to surfers who don't live here, don't have a business, or vote here?"

"Who's going to listen to a dead old man?" said Joe, clicking his cheeks, and pressing his thumb stump on the control box button. "Up!"

"No," moaned Koolner, obediently standing up.

"Uh, who says you can teach an old dog new tricks," said Joe, giving off a fixed glare. "I'm taking you to your home break."

Slick and Purpus went back to his place. They were carrying their boards. They wore swimshorts and damp sweatshirts. They found a note tacked to the front door.

"You leave something for me?" asked Slick, putting down his board and the cooler.

"No," replied Purpus, putting his stick beside Slick's.

They read the note:

> *I want to talk to you. Go to the phone van parked off the road by the treatment plant. By the Adamson estate house.*
>
> *Surfer Joe*
> P.S. *Bring your kook friend.*

"Let's got back to The One and check it out," said Slick, looking at his cousin.

The two went down to the Coast Highway and walked past The Wall. The Gidget Invitational contest work crews were setting up bunting, scaffolds, and tents on the beach. The sizzling and crumbling Malibu waves mixed with the man-made sounds of hammering, clanging steel pipes, and a gas-powered generator. Two fifty-foot balloons were half inflated.

Slick and Purpus found a phone company van parked off the

road, partially concealed in the bushes by a utility pole near the Adamson estate house. The van's back doors were ajar. The inside was lighted.

Slick tapped on the back door and said, "Yo, Joe."

"What do you think he wants to see me for?" nervously whispered Purpus.

"Well, you *wanted* to meet the legend himself," said Slick, smirking. He opened the door. "Joe?" Slick poked his head inside. "Bitchen little pad."

Purpus followed his cousin into the van. They bent down and stepped around the bags of soybeans and oranges, checked out the closet, fridge, the TV screen and the video tape machine.

Slick bent down over a stack of red flyers piled on the floor and read aloud, "'Protest Malibu's Professional Surfing Contests.'" He paused. "I should have known Joe was putting these contest protest things up."

"Hmmmmm," said Purpus, seeing the leather-bound books on the shelf. He went over to them. "All classics. Plutarch, Stendal, London, Conrad, Yeats, Flaubert, Thoreau, Farley, Melville, Kipling, Hadley, Shakespeare, Hemingway, Reiss, and Twain."

"Well, you know, surfers are suppose to be stupid," said Slick, who came over.

"I think this is a journal" said Purpus, pulling out a bulging, large scrapbook. Skip flipped through it. The entries were meticulously printed in blue ink. Between every other page were photographs of waves, lava, remote desert, and long stretches of empty beaches. There were diagrams of waves, weather charts and below them map coordinates.

"What's on the last page?" asked Slick, reaching across and turning to the end of the book. They read the final entry:

> I'm the dream every surfer has, I searched for waves my entire life and rode them. I followed an endless summer around the world and found the ultimate wave. But then the dream changed into a reality. My Big Sea turned into my Big C—cancer. The sun and polluted water killed me. My dream killed me. But, a dream can kill two ways.

"Sounds like one of his scams," impassively said Slick. He took the journal, turned a the pages and skimmed a few passages.

"It's pretty interesting," said Skip.

"Real surfers don't think like this," dismissively said Slick, closing the book. "This is just Joe's hustle to buy into his myth. This is a book for kooks."

"Check this out," said Purpus, pulling out a video cassette that said 'Gidg Must Die'.

"Makes about as much sense as everything else," said Slick, unimpressed.

Purpus plugged the tape into the VCR and turned on the set. Surfer Joe walked on the screen. He wore a swimsuit, and a belt which had a huge circular buckle with a button in the center of it. He carried an Uzi. Joe tapped his sunglasses, tilted his head, clicked his cheek, and said, "The day of the Malibu contest I'm going to take off on the ultimate clean-up wave." Joe, pointed to the disc on the belt, "On my Aloha Wave, I'm going to press this button. It will transmit a   signal that will take out all the kooks, and, uh, clean out the shores. It's my way of making amends. You see, the world is crazy and it's killing everything and I'm going to kick out before it closes out on me and destroys itself. I'm taking all the bad with me. I will find my redemption on my Aloha Wave. It's time to even down everything."

The screen went blank. In the darkness on the screen they saw Joe's figure reflected behind them.

"Yes, my friends, I see you have complicated matters some," said Joe, holding a pistol.

"Why did you tell us to come?" asked Purpus.

"You left us a note," added Slick.

"No, I didn't leave you a note but I know who did," said Joe, tilting his head and smiling. "Yes, Slick and my kook friend, you two are in for a real expression session."

"It's time to surf the Malibu you made, Koolner," said Joe, removing the old man's blindfold.

Koolner uncomfortably found himself standing upright on a longboard. His shoes were fiberglassed to its deck. The board teetered over the edge of a chute, which angled from the top of the highest septic tank and ended into an open sludge tank below it. The old man uncomfortably looked: the slide ended into a lively brown ooze at the bottom.

"Can you guys see all right?" asked Surfer Joe, looking down to his right at Slick and Purpus, who sat beside each other on the concrete incline between the two tanks. Their wrists duct-taped behind their backs.

"Don't mind us," replied Slick, looking upwards at Joe, who stood on the platform with Koolner.

"Yeah, go right ahead," added Purpus, trying to blow flies away from his face.

Surfer Joe wheeled around, advanced to Koolner and said, "Now, old man, your world is being taken away from you!" Joe gestured to the ocean and the hills. "I've got everything wired. The bungalows, the pier, the condos, the restaurants, the boutiques, t-shirt stands, and even your mansion!" He paused. "Victory dance." The three men watched Surfer Joe boogie against the moon in the cool Malibu night.

"Joe, you can't kill all those innocent people," said Slick.

Surfer Joe stopped his victory dance and innocently asked, "Why not? They're kooks!"

"Yeah, but still..." Slick slowly said, without much conviction.

A female figure strolled up the incline.

"You!" gasped Koolner, stunned. "The Gidget!"

"Gidg...Gidg...Gidg..." sputtered Joe.

Joe was back in the Black Tube, crouching down on his board, the dark lip pitching over him.

Koolner clasped his hands, laughed and exuberantly said, "Joe, don't you see it? The Gidget had this whole thing planned. I'm not the one you want. If she set you up in 1959, what do you think she plans to do to you in 1994?"

"Gidg...Gidg...Gidg..." sputtered Joe, quickly ducking within the cylindrical tube and seeing Koolner's face through the blackness.

"Joe," sharply clipped Koolner, "Joe, I can tell you exactly how your father died."

A gunshot shattered the glassy Black Tube around Joe. It burst into sharp shards and disappeared. Joe twitched, as if the bullet from the past that ripped through his father's skull had ricocheted into him. Joe tried to regain his composure. He breathed deeply, clicked his cheek, tapped his sunglasses, and tilted his head.

"Did you hear me? I know how your father died," whispered Koolner, like a prayer.

"You killed him," confidently said Joe.

"Please don't hurt me, please, please, please," implored Koolner, sobbing. "I'll give you anything, tell you anything, please.

Not me, please, please, oh, please. Don't do this!"

"Uh, you're pathetic,"said Joe, lifting the bottom of the finless board and shoving it down the slide.

"Not me," bellowed Koolner.

"Surf's up," said Joe.

"I can't surf!" screamed Koolner, struggling to keep his balance as he slid down the chute. "Noooooooooo!"

Koolner splattered into the tank. The longboard's nose purled into the pool of sludge, and flipped. Flies flew up. The old man was submerged within the black ooze. His flailing rocked the board from side to side, but he couldn't turn it over. A huge carpet of flies settled back on the rolling surface. The pool eventually stopped stirring

"Shit happens," said Joe.

Slick and Purpus were lying on the floor of Joe's van. They were tied back to back, wrapped head-to-toe with several layers of silver duct tape.

"You know, uh, Slick, if I didn't take you out, uh," said Surfer Joe, removing the panel from the closet. "Uh, if you had won that contest instead of me, you'd be here and I'd be where you are."

"We can still switch," grunted Slick, who sarcastically added, "After all, there's only *one* King of Malibu."

"Yeah," said Joe. He found four sticks of taped-together dynamite connected to a flash-powder fuse. He asked himself, "Where did this come from?"

"Sure you have enough dynamite?" facetiously asked Slick.

"I buy them by the case," said Joe. "That way I don't run out." He put the dynamite back. "Actually that one is left over."

"Must have—"

"Oblivion costs, Slick." said Joe, reaching down into the closet and pulling out a gym bag with the money. "I think $80,000 will get you there." Joe put the bag on the floor. "You won't need as much money as me. I had my image. And the boys with their cameras and notepads followed me wherever I went. They wanted to interview me, take a picture, and expose my new surfing spots. Man, those kooks found me wherever I was." He added in an unusual vulnerable admission. "I kinda asked for it, I guess."

"Pardon me while I cry you a river," said Slick, but then the cash registered. "Wait, you're really giving me money. Let me—"

"Slick, you're not listening, you need the money to achieve the oblivion," rapidly said Joe. "Oblivion. That's what Malibu was. Uh, no one cared about it but us." He took the map from the closet and unfolded it on the floor near Slick's head. Joe gleefully said, "But the boys with their cameras didn't find me *here*."

"There?" dubiously asked Slick, looking at the red-circled area. Water spurted out of his nostrils onto the map. "Brain waves."

"More like a tidal pool," said Surfer Joe, smiling, wiping the map, and pointing to the location. "No hotels or wharves. Just natives and it's all primitive and back into its essence. And when the swells come, uh, they don't last for days, uh, they last for months! And I'm not talking about five-wave sets. I'm talking about hours of waves. There's a perfect right that just peels and goes. Sometimes the left goes off. It gets hollow and tubes, but it's kinda like Sunset, real fast and almost impossible to make. And the spot takes any swell. And you know what? No sharks."

"None?" asked Slick.

"They're eaten by salt-water crocodiles," said Joe, smiling. "So, they're afraid."

"Salt water crocodiles!" exclaimed Slick. "I'd rather take my chances with a shark. With a shark you can fight with dignity."

"Yes my friend, but every dream has a killer attached to it in this perfect world," said Joe, pulling an Uzi from the closet. He took out huge ammo belts and the circular detonation transmitter. He put them in a long canvas bag that contained his board.

"Still it's another Malibu," cautiously interrupted Purpus.

"Did I hear the call of the kook?" asked Surfer Joe.

"He's a bro, Joe," quickly said Slick with obvious concern.

"I know how you perceive me," said Joe, speaking to Purpus. "You see me as someone who contributed to the fall of his own wall. How does that separate me from you? I wanted to beat the kooks at their own game and still surf, I was wrong, but I was young and dumb. And Slick? He tried all the ego-assuaging too. He became a pro, hoping he could beat the kook world and never have a day job so he could surf. And you? Every wave is a search. You're hoping you can find something out about my Malibu to escape from the kook world. So you tell me what I did wrong."

"You surfed in The Gidget."

"Gidg...Gidg...Gidg..." sputtered Joe, closing his eyes and concentrating. He wanted to keep The Black Tube away.

"Now you did it," sighed Slick, rolling his eyes.

"Gidg...Gidg...Gidg..." continued Joe, but he felt the image of the tube receding.

"What did I say? What did I say?" helplessly plead Purpus. "I just said Gid—"

"Noooo," said Surfer Joe, shaking off the image's hold upon him. He shivered, but firmly stated, "Everyone has a self-destructive kook within them. The kook within me wanted to be known, you don't want to be known, do you?"

"I just want to surf and see what comes out of that," said Purpus. "I don't want a thing."

"That's more about you than I wanted to know, gremmie," said Joe, putting duct tape over Purpus' mouth. "You can have the journal, all the flow charts, and waves theories. Use it, you write a book with it. You want a Malibu—well, just remember, you needed me to find it. I have a place in all this." He tapped his sunglasses. "Think of it, my kook friend, a natural place, a tropical spot, a remote area. Where you can surf with the wave and not against the people. Where you can find a style." Joe tilted his head. "And you'd be part of it, my friend. Slick will take you. Cause you see, a perfect ride isn't truly a perfect ride unless your buddy watches you get it." He paused. "Surfing by yourself can get real old." Joe clicked his cheek. "And when you're there, you'll know what I lost. I'm giving you perfection. Let's see if you can avoid the snake of temptation to make more money so you can be freer. If you can do it, you made the hardest section." He twitched. "I couldn't make it. I'm trying to make up for that now. I will make up for it." Joe rapidly moved his fingers about. "If I had the chance to do it all over again, you know what I'd really do?"

"Untie us?" hopefully asked Slick.

"I would have run *her* off the beach the first time she wanted to surf," said Joe, talking quickly. "I'd do it. God, how I'd do it." He glared at the past. He body tensed. "All I wanted to do is surf, Slick. If none of this stuff happened, I'd be just like you."

"Concept," added Slick. "But a real step up for you."

Joe put the bag of money behind a sack of soybeans. "Don't tell her it's there."

"I thought you trusted Gid—"

"No names!" Joe said sharply, holding up his hands.

Slick, scrunched down his eyebrows, smiled and asked "You still love her?"

"There's no love," rapidly said Surfer Joe with an edge. His head twitched. "That was before that book. Before the kooks! Anything after that isn't really love. Love was before." Joe added bitterly. "Women, they're nothing but trouble. They're only good for one thing. If I need them I just go to Singapore for a week and fuck my brains out. But I can do without them. And I can always use my hand, and sometimes I can do without that too." Joe twitched. "It's her, her, her! She's always been the lie, Slick." Joe took out a baggie from the closet. It was filled with white powder. He dug the long yellowed nail of his forefinger into the drug. "But I have a little surprise. A little pharmaceutical aid for her sleeping needs. After that, I can establish my beach head tomorrow."

There was a loud boom from the ocean, even louder than the one Slick and Crispy heard the night before.

"It's going to get bigger," said Joe.

"Obvee," flatly said Slick.

Joe put duct tape over Slick's mouth, listened to the waves, narrowed his eyes and intently said, "You know, I've always *hated* the ocean."

Surfer Joe and The Gidget were having a private luau. He fed the campfire. A sand dune enclosed their oasis of the past. Joe's board bag laid sideways in the sand. They were on a private beach behind a vacant house, a few thousand feet south of the Malibu Creek rivermouth.

"It's just as I imagined it would be," said The Gidget, lying on a towel, resting on her elbows. She wore a tank-top bathing suit.

"Really," said Joe, clicking his cheek sitting beside her.

The Gidget said, "Joey, did you really mean what you said back there?"

"Uh, I mean everything, uh, but what particular point do you wish to raise?"

"Did you really mean it when you talked about wiring this whole place up to explode—"

"I was goofing to wig the old man out," said Surfer Joe, waving her off. "I wanted Koolner to leave this world on a lie."

"Let's just leave."

"We will, on a wave made for both of us," distantly said Joe, taking out a bottle and opening it with a corkscrew. "Have some vino. A 1945 Chateau Laffitte I liberated from your stepdad's cellar." Joe furtively poured the Bordeaux over his yellowed forefinger. The powdered drug under his nail dissolved into The Gidget's wine. "It might taste a little flinty with a touch of cassis."

"Joey, what if everything was gone and it was just the way it was and we knew then what we know now," said The Gidget, stretching out her body on the towel.

"I *know* now what I knew then, it didn't help me."

"Wouldn't that be wonderful?"

"Somewhere I guess."

"Maybe if we close out eyes and kiss and open them we'll be back there."

They kissed. The Gidget opened her eyes. Joe's were still closed. God, she thought, he's really trying to make this happen. She quickly closed her eyes. Joe opened his eyes.

He was disappointed.

Crispy got Slick back. The old man needed a drink. Actually, he deserved one. Especially after carting all these goods from the cave to Slick's place. It took him hours. His insides felt like dried mud, curling up in small sections. His body independently craved the moisture of a drink. He looked around Slick's small three-room bungalow. It was a trove. The kitchen counter and sink were stacked with numerous Chumash artifacts—rocks, pestles, shelled necklaces. Intricately woven baskets were piled to the bathroom ceiling. The floors were packed with cardboard boxes, which contained Spanish gold, pearls, and jewelry. He wanted to celebrate. But there wasn't any beer in the fridge. He hoped Slick would show up to buy him a drink.

"I made it up to you, Slick," said Crispy, sadly looking around the room. "Fuck, I hit my lottery, and I can't cash any of this shit in for a six-pack. Where the fuck am I going to get a drink, now?"

The front door slammed open against the wall.

"I bought some more tequila!" said a drunk and cute blonde. "Let's get raging."

Crispy looked up and said, "I'm not Slick."

"Obvee," said the girl. She was a fine young thing wearing bluejean shorts and a white t-shirt that ended just above her navel, which had a metal hook embedded in it. She wasn't wearing a bra. Crispy could see it was cold outside. "Like, where is he?"

"I don't know," said Crispy. "It's ten o' clock, I thought he'd be here by now." He moistened his lips and said, "Can I have a hit off that?"

"For sure," said the girl, who bounced over and sat next to the old man. "You moving in here or something?"

"Oh yeah," said Crispy, taking a long pull without tasting it. The liquor soaked out the dried mud feeling. He felt moist again. His eyes became flatter.

The girl leaned toward him and said, "Your eyes, I mean, your face looks hard, but your eyes, they show there's sweetness inside you. Are you a surfer?"

"Always," said Crispy, who felt a stirring within that he usually suppressed because there was never the proper outlet. Crispy knew what he looked like to women, and if she was interested in him, nothing about his personality could stop her, so, he cut to the chase. "Can I interest you in a wrist corsage?"

The girl looked down. Her face stretched out to show how impressed she was, and her eyes showed a mixture of eager terror and hungry readiness.

"Concept!" she said, giggling. She lifted off her top.

Crispy watched her firm breasts wobble from side to side. They didn't sag. They swayed, settled up high, and held. The old man smiled and took another tasteless tequila pull from the bottle. He could get behind it.

Chapter eight

Aloha Wave

Dead had arrived.

The direction was Dead South from a New Zealand groundswell. It traveled a long distance. The swell had time to unroll, smooth out, and build its clout. You could see it coming. The creased lines of swell extended toward the horizon, far beyond the kelp, further than anyone had ever seen them stretch. This was Dead South. These waves were, thick, ripe and nasty. They wrapped around the outside reef, flexing like bulging muscles. A majestic ugliness lurked within them. Their shoulders resembled huge slanted roofs fringed at their peak with snow. Even the foam was brutal. The white curls crashed behind the walls, as if they were storm clouds trying to overrun, level and consume the waves. Each advancing wave rumbled like a jet engine. The warm west offshore wind made the throwing feathered tips flare in a mist of arcing rainbows, which drizzled and disappeared like technicolor fumes. The mounded backs of the waves passed under the pier and rattled the boardwalk. The air reeked of salt. This was a solid Dead South swell. The ocean was corduroy and big. The sets marched in. Every wave was progressively bigger than the one before it. They spread out like a set of ascending steps. Each time a surfer scratched over one wave, they found themselves in an even deeper but narrowing sudsy trough, staring up at an even larger wave ready to pitch and crush down upon them. Some surfers couldn't paddle over these breaking waves. They got caught inside. Surfboards snapped in half. Leashes broke like licorice strings. Loose boards were pushed by the foam sideways to the shore. The air was rent with more howls, hoots, and screams for Jesus than a revival meeting. And the waves continued to advance, brutally combing and mowing down anyone who was in the way. Surfers took deep breaths, bailed off their sticks, and dove underwater. The more fortunate proned-out, clung desperately to their boards, and somehow rode the bouncing white water to the dry safety of the shore. Eight to ten surfers still managed to take off on each of the waves, colliding with one another, dropping in front of one another, swearing at one another, and crashing into others who were trying to paddle up between the diagonal riders on the shoulders. Those that remained, determinedly paddled out. It was no longer just an ocean. No longer just Malibu. The Dead South turned the once familiar surface into an unknown territory filled with a moving landscape of rolling peaks and curved valleys and ledge-crumbling canyons. It was another world. A different realm. A living frontier.

It was the day for a legend to die.

Dead had arrived.

Surfer Joe scanned the kookfest. Two fifty-foot helium balloons, a beer can and a hot dog, were tied to the scaffolding. They floated above the judge's platform, which was built fifteen feet above the beach. On the stage, under a tent, judgmental fat men sat with clipboards behind folding tables. They wore straw hats, Hawaiian shirts, shorts, and sandals. All of them were pale, loud, hungover, and stupid looking. The banner above the stage said "The Gidget Invitational Surf Reunion sponsored by Devine Foam." A surf oldie "Pipeline" by The Chantay's thumped its bassline and splashed out its wet glissandos through the huge speakers behind the stage. Along the beach were concession stands selling t-shirts, or preparing tacos, burgers, and dogs. In the crowd, babes from a popular TV show "Baywatch" and numerous bikini models wandered around, their huge breasts almost had more lift than the helium balloons. Indignant contest surfers stood about in numbered sleeveless jerseys.

Fat guys from all over the state strutted in the surf club shirts and hats. Safely behind the lapping reach of the waves, in a roped-off area, were dry surf magazine photographers with four-foot long lensed cameras on tripods, as well as with TV crews, surf film producers gathering contest footage to use on videos, and drunk friends of contest organizers with all-access passes. The parking lot was filled with restored Woodies from the forties and fifties—all covered with surf stickers on their windows. The beach was almost packed with more people than sand. Upright longboards leaned against every inch of the Malibu Wall. There two-hundred surfers in the water, Joe showed his gap-toothed grin, his protest posters worked. He'd definitely have a high-kill ratio.

"Uh, are the Beach Boys here?" asked the slouch-postured Joe, gingerly holding two modern longboards. "Uh, I was looking forward to personally telling them how much their music has meant to me over the years."

"All surfers out of the water for the contest, please!" commanded the fat man into the bullhorn, standing on the judge's platform. He was too caught up in his problems to notice Joe. The fat man wore a neon lime cap that said "Contest director." The navel of his gut protruded underneath an Hawaiian shirt. He lowered his bullhorn and turned to see a man with black hair and mustache, who wore a contest hat, bathing trunks, sandals, and a windbreaker marked "Security" on its front pocket.

"What do you want?" asked the exasperated director.

"These are the sticks for the Beach Boys, my friend, all waxed up too," said Joe.

"They won't be here for hours," snapped the fat man. "Put them over by the awning."

Joe returned, stood beside the fat man and said, "Uh, I'd say this is quite a turnout."

"Some jerk's been printing these damn things up telling everybody the truth," snapped the director, shaking a red flyer. "Now, how the hell can we have our contest? Look at all those surfers. If we go out there and touch them they'll sue us for assault. Christ, everyone has a frigging video camera." He paused. "We need a miracle to clear out the water."

"Uh, I'm your miracle," calmly said Joe, tapping his sunglasses as he descended the steps. He picked up his board bag and walked to the ocean.

A middle-aged kook in the crowd recognized him.

"Hey, aren't you Surfer Joe?" a fat guy in an Hawaiian shirt eagerly asked him. "Would you sign my program?" He fumbled for a pen.

Joe briskly walked to the edge of the beach, and put down his bag in the sand. He quickly removed his cap, mustache, and wig. Joe unzipped the bag, and carefully slid out his father's longboard. It was fitted with two options: the first one was a wax mold sculpted on the deck near the tip, housing an Uzi; the second, was a jagged series of six-inch razor blades fiberglassed to the edge of the board's nose. Joe removed his jacket, across his bare chest was a rappelling harness containing ammo belts loaded with clips.

"I see this isn't a good time for you," the fat kook meekly warbled, seeing the weaponry. He backpedaled and ran away.

"You saved me a bullet," gravely said Joe.

The air horn honked.

"All surfers must please leave the water, now!" shouted the events director over the bullhorn.

Joe pulled out a wide belt from the travel bag. He reached down and gently removed a silver disc. It had red button in the center. He checked the detonation transmitter. The batteries were working. The six-inch diameter disc had two curved hooks on its top and bottom. Joe attached the device by sliding the belt through the four curved hooks. He put the belt on, adjusting the transmitter so it was on his side. He took a few steps, the disc jiggled and slid along the waist strap toward the rear part of the belt by his back. Joe slid it to his side.

The next song on the sound system began. It was a tune called "Surfer Joe" by The Surfaris.

"Uh, the only surf song I ever liked, uh," said Joe, tucking the board under his arm, and bouncing on the balls of his feet to the music's beat. "Even though they stole my name."

The Surfaris classic tune went:

Down in Doheny where the surfers all go
Lives a big bleach blondie named Surfer Joe
He's got a green surfboard and a Woody to match
When he's driving the freeways, man, is he hard to catch

"Yes my friends, uh, I love it when life imitates art," said Joe, paddling out in his Malibu.

Slick and Purpus were still tightly tied back to back with duct tape, looking like a two-headed silver cocoon with four feet. They heard a car park outside and footsteps crunch on gravel toward them. The van's doors rattled. A hand wielding a large silver blade poked through the opening doors. It was The Gidget. She was wearing a tank top bathing suit and smoking a cigarette. Her hair was uncombed and her make-up looked like child's art project.

"Up for a dawn session?" she asked, using the knife and to cut the duct-tape gags loose.

"We've got to stop him," said Slick, gasping. "He's going to kill everybody."

"The bastard put something in my drink," said The Gidget, exhaling smoke. "I woke up and he was gone. I feel like crap." She looked about and asked, "Where's Joe?"

"He's at the contest, Gidget—"

"The Gidget." She sneered and deeply inhaled through her cigarette. "I hate this Gidget stuff. I'm not The Gidget!" She slowly growled, "For years, every day of my life I have to listen to kooks ask me about Malibu, ask me about Surfer Joe, ask me if people hate me for ruining Malibu. I'm not The Gidget. That's someone else's fictional character. The Gidget doesn't exist." She narrowed her eyes. "When all this is done I'll have everything, I don't have to depend on a stepfather or Joe, or anyone! I'll have my life back."

"We have to stop..." said Slick, his voice trailed off. He asked, "What do you mean by 'when all this is done'?"

She brought the knife against Slick's throat and rasped, "You were suppose to back up my stepfather's story. You can't do that anymore." Slick stared straight into her eyes. The Gidget dropped the knife and said, "Shit, I need someone else to do this."

"I always thought you were a yuppie," said Slick.

"Why don't you just leave us here?" asked Purpus. "We don't care what the fuck you guys do."

"Oh yeah, I believe that," scoffed The Gidget, going into the closet. She found the dynamite. The Gidget examined the grayish-powdered fuse. It was eight-feet in length. She nodded.

"He's got everything wired—"

"The bastard lied to me," said The Gidget, blowing out smoke. She looked around. "But this will do for now."

The Gidget opened the metal grill that separated the driver's cab from the back of the van. She placed the dynamite in the front seat. She briefly pondered leaving the fuse and the explosive, but the fuse was too long, and if she overlapped it, the fuse might burn across a looped section, ignite it closer to the dynamite, and go off before she got away. She left the deadly package in the cab, threaded the fuse through the grill work, and closed the panel. Then, she pulled the fuse until it reached the rear of the van.

"You can't get to the dynamite," said The Gidget, using her cigarette to light the fuse. "And you can't blow it out." She blew on it. "Peace." She slammed the door. They heard her car peel out, scattering gravel that pinged on the van.

They watched the fuse burn past them.

"Jesus!" wheezed Slick.

"Oh shit!" shrieked Purpus.

The two duct-taped surfers rapidly squirmed toward the burning fuse.

"Just lay on the thing," said Purpus.

They did. It still burned underneath them and kept going.

"Shit, it's burning too fast, move!" said Slick.

"Spit on it!" shouted Purpus.

"I can't get it up," said Slick, working his tongue over his dried mouth.

"Fuck it let me try!" said Purpus, pulling the opposite way.

Their frantic twisting ripped apart their silver cocoon. They broke free from each other. But, their arms were still individually bound with duct tape. They crawled over the fuse, trying to blow it out. The fuse kept burning.

Slick and Purpus pleaded, "Please Go—"

Salt water suddenly gushed out of both their noses like a faucet. It splattered on the dry fuse. The orange spark turned black. The fuse was out.

"Score!" shouted Slick, laughing.

"Yes, yes, yes!" said Purpus.

They heard "Pipeline" from the contest area.

"Where's that knife?" asked Slick, rolling back to the closet. He found the blade, laid on his back, and cut the tape between his wrists, freeing himself.

"Do me."

"This is my wave, Skip," said Slick, getting up and ripping the tape off his body. "This is about Joe and me now."

He left the knife on the floor by Purpus and ran to The Bu.

"Will you assholes clear out of the fucking water for my surf contest," whined the fat man with the bullhorn. He felt a tug and heard a snap. "Hey!"

"Thanks," said Slick, yanking the binoculars off the contest director's chest.

"What's up?" asked the fat man, recognizing Slick.

Slick looked through the binoculars and anxiously scanned the ocean. He searched for Joe amid the horde of surfers in the water. *There.* Just disappearing over the hump of a wave. Slick saw Joe paddle with his left leg up. He handed the binoculars to the director.

"I need a ride," said Slick, grabbing the modern longboard from under an awning. and tucking the orange stick under his arm.

"Slick, you can't take that board," said the director. "That's for the Beach Boys."

"They don't surf," said Slick, running down the platform, across the strand of sand, and passing Crispy.

"The Big One is coming," shouted Crispy, swaying. He held a paper bag containing a thirty-two-ounce bottle of beer. "There's a wave out there with your name on it, Slick."

Slick jumped, threw his board underneath him, and hit the water paddling. He looked outside at a set wrapping way beyond the kelp line. He had never seen a set form that far out. The last wave in the clean-up set had to be Surfer Joe's Aloha Wave.

"The Big One!" Slick heard Crispy declare from the shore. "The Big One is coming!"

Surfer Joe
Now look at him go
Surfer, Surfer, Surfer Joe
Go man go
Oh, oh, Surfer Joe

Rasta Head and Booger Ring paddled their shortboards alongside Joe, and popped off at him.

"Valley go home," nasally snarled the Rasta Head through his broken nose. "We're not leaving, a contest permit only entitles you to the beach not the water."

"What's with the outfit? You going to arrest us?" jeered Booger Ring, clawing at the rolling water. His right hand was in a cast and sealed with plastic wrap.

The shortboarders abuse basted Joe's anger. Joe hummed The Surfaris' tune and reached for the Uzi.

"Outside! Outside" yelled several surfers, but it wasn't a shout of exultation, it seemed more like a cry of retreat.

Joe pulled his hand away from the weapon. He arched off his board and saw a massive gun-metal colored hump behind the set. It was his Aloha Wave.

Inside...

"Shit!" growled Slick, paddling hard and angrily, his hands digging and gouging water out the rising shoulder.

His longboard was vertical to the wave's towering face. There was six-feet of water beneath him and a three feet of a bright watery overhang above him. Slick looked like he was paddling his board up the face of an avalanching cliff. The peak was creaming white with foam, hissing. It was just on the verge of pitching him backwards. He didn't want to get caught inside, if he did, Slick would never be in position to take off behind Joe on the Aloha Wave. Slick was not to be denied. He windmilled his arms. The wave started to throw. He punched the board's pointed nose through the translucent lip.

"Aoooah!" Slick growled.

Slick squirted out of the wave's massive back. He spurted into the air like a jumping fish. The bottom of the board slapped when it hit the water. The wave crumbled behind him like someone bombed it. White spray blew and stung his face. It was like getting caught in a sudden blizzard. He blinked rapidly, clearing his vision. He didn't believe what was coming toward him.

"Hello!" shrieked Slick, his eyes widening.

It was The Big One. The set wave of all Malibu set waves sucked up the valley of water in front of him, adding to its height. The moving slab rose into a bruised-tinted half dome. Slick couldn't see any sky, all he saw was water growing around him. It was the biggest, nastiest Malibu wave Slick had ever seen. And he wanted every ounce of it. He spun his board around and paddled. Water ledged beneath him. A force surged around him, pushed the tail up, tilted the board, and violently heaved Slick down its steep crevice as the wave curled up behind him. It was as if the ocean was trying to pull itself out from underneath him. The offshore wind pressed against the turquoise wave, hollowing it out, and webbing the rising eight-foot banked wall with curved support beams. Slick carved across it. The right rail thumped a steady beat against the shoulder's watery ribs. Spray crackled over the board's pointed nose like a white blaze. The fin hummed from the speed of water wrapping around it. And the curl sizzled and pounded behind him. Fifty feet down the line, Slick saw Surfer Joe and a few shortboarders take off. Slick knew Joe wouldn't look back, because he never expected anyone to take off this deep behind him.

Slick softly growled, "You're on *my* wave now, Joe."

He went down to Huntington Beach on week
For the annual surfer's convention meet
He was hanging five and walking the nose
And when the meet was over the trophy was Joe's

Joe grabbed his weapon, and stood up as he slid down the wave. The two shortboarder took off with him. Rasta Head to Joe's right, dropped in front him, and Booger Ring behind him, dropping to Joe's left.

"Back off kook!" shouted Booger Ring.

"Koooooooooooooooook!" ululated Joe stepping hard on the board's tail and bringing it around.

The razors on the board's nose ripped open the youth's throat; its reddened wound looked like fresh chili. Blood spurted and the buzzcut punk dropped.

Surfer Joe
Now look at him go
Surfer, Surfer, Surfer Joe
Go man go
Oh, oh, Surfer Joe

"Nice kick out," proclaimed Joe, his eyes glazing over. He fired the Uzi at the dreadlock shortboarder.

Rasta Head's chest splattered, as if someone had thrown raspberry jelly on him. Joe danced a little to the Surfaris' song. The kid fell.

"Party wave!" shouted Joe, laughing as he randomly fired his weapon at people in the water. His eyes glazed with power. "I should have thought of this years ago." He reloaded and fired again.

A bullhorn voice said from the shore, "Will the surfer with the automatic weapon please leave the water immediately. Will—"

"Critics!" bellowed Joe, putting a round into the beach.

Spectators fell, ran, ducked. Cameras dropped to the ground. The press objectively scattered. One bullet hit the plastic explosive in one of the longboards. The gasoline cans Joe placed last night under the supports worked. The judge's platform blew up in a round fireball centered with blackness. The huge inflated beer can and hot dog floated up into the sky, as if the Supreme Being had placed an order to eat and watch the show.

"Die valleys die!" screeched Joe, casually and accurately firing at the people who desperately tried to paddle away.

Joe trimmed down the line into the shallower water. The breaking wave accelerated and curved deeper within itself. The shoulder rose double overhead, dredging up the dark silt from the bottom. The wave turned from bluish-green to blackness. The lip threw out several feet, curled over, and formed a cylinder. Joe pulled into it.

The Black Tube had arrived.

The chant began, "Gidget must die, Gidget must die, Gidget must die."

"Yes, my friends, I'm coming," he whispered to the guardians of his imagined sanctuary.

Crispy and Purpus were sprawled on the sand, using the dead body of a surf photographer for cover. Most of the film crew were on their knees, recording Slick chasing Surfer Joe.

"Curtain call," said Crispy, pointing to the fifteen-foot long sheet of water throwing out and forming a spiraling cylinder that wound into itself.

When Surfer Joe pulled into the tube, Slick was just ten feet behind him, but it was a critical ten feet.

"The tube's going to close before he can make it!" said Purpus, pointing at the darkening black-sand dredging barrel.

"Slick's got to do a shortboard move," said Crispy, nudging Purpus, chuckling. "He'll make it then."

Slick saw the dark tube sealing shut. There was only one maneuver he could make to enter the tube. And every longboarding muscle of his body resisted it, but he had to go for it.

"Butt-wiggling shortboarder piece-of-shit move," Slick mumbled to himself, rapidly pumping the board with his legs.

Slick quickly snapped to his left, shooting out a spray from the tail. He drove back to the deepest and lowest curved part of the pitching wave, angrily torqued his body, and cranked a hard bottom turn. He flipped the board around to the right and shot vertically straight up the curved face toward the heaving lip. Slick timed this move so the bottom of the board smacked the pitching top of the wave. He bent down on one knee and grabbed the outside rail. The force of the lip tossed him into the air. Slick held tightly to his board and turned it so the nose was pointed downward into the whirlpool-swirling opening of the cylinder below.

"Gyro fucking skateboarding geek," he mumbled, threading into the spiraling tunnel.

The tube closed behind him. He and Surfer Joe were locked in its black room together. It was the last room they would share.

Surfer Joe joined Uncle Sam's Marines today
They stationed him at Pendleton not far away
They cut off his big blonde locks I'm told
And when they went on maneuvers, Joe caught cold

Joe was within The Black Tube.

"Gidget must die, Gidget must die, Gidget must die..." urged the voices. They spoke louder and faster.

Joe was as deep within The Malibu as he could ever get. Ahead a white light flooded through The Black Tube's opening, illuminating the curved wall. It seemed as if the bright beam belonged to a higher spiritual plane from another world.

"Malibu, take me," pleaded Joe, reaching to press the button to achieve his salvation.

The transmitter wasn't there! He looked down. Somehow during Joe's ride, the silver disc had jiggled and slid on its clasps along the belt and worked its way to the middle of his back.

Joe panicked, dropping the Uzi. He struggled to press the button. But the shoulder-ammo harness restricted Joe's arm movements. He strained, stretched, and struggled. The stump of his left thumb was a mere half digit away from the button.

"Gidget must die! Gidget must die! Gidget must die!" chanted the voices, faster and higher.

The opening ahead of Joe closed. The light of salvation was gone. Behind him, Joe heard the a board slapping the wall of water. The black figure, flashed Joe, looking back down the dark swirling cylinder.

"Noooooo," Joe whined like a fifteen year old boy. "Please, please, please!"

"I love payback!" roared Slick, tucking under the curl and bearing down on Joe. He jumped backwards, shoving his feet hard on the tail's deck, launching the board at its target.

Joe blubbered in a tantrum-like rage, "There's only one King of Mal—"

The warhead ding solidly connected with Joe's forehead.

"Score!" said Slick, tumbling.

The blast imploded into The Black Tube, pummeling Slick down into the roiling water. His ears ached. He rolled along the sandy bottom. Slick opened his eyes and saw Surfer Joe's purplish-red coil disappear in swirling wave. Joe made his final section.

The song finished out with:

Surfer Joe
Now look at him go
Surfer, Surfer, Surfer Joe
Go man go
Oh, oh, Surfer Joe
Oh, oh, poor Joe!

"There he is," said Purpus, pointing Slick out to Crispy. They ran toward him.

Slick stood up to his waist in the shore pound. His body bled from various cuts. He gasped for breath and looked around. The platform was on fire. People screamed. In the water, surfboards became floating tombstones, anchored with leash cords to the dead below. News crews filmed the partial devastation. But everything else was intact. The mansions. The pier's pilings. The fast-food

170

franchises. The hotels. The cottages. The Colony. The boutiques. Tee-shirt shops. Koolner's sewage treatment plant. Actually, outside of the dead and the fires it seemed like a typical Saturday.

"Where the fuck did that explosion come from?" asked a dazed Slick, his ears filled with a long beeping tone

"Nice wave, shortboarder, you pulled air!" said Crispy, laughing. "You shredded th—"

Sounds like muffled firecrackers came from a distant hill. Crispy's right shoulder shoved forward. He fell face down on the beach. The beer bottle flew out of its bag. Several bullets kicked up sand and splashed the shorebreak.

"Shit!" yipped Purpus, ducking behind the photographer's corpse on the berm.

"Fuck!" shouted Slick, diving underwater.

The gunshots made a flock of pigeons fly from the roof of Koolner's mansion. The Gidget was concealed within a snipers nest constructed from several large cardboard boxes of books on Koolner's mansion deck. Three slightly bent shell casings were neatly lined up at her feet.

"Damn," grunted The Gidget, smacking the weapon. She rested the base of the rifle's barrel on the porch railing.

A voice, a very familiar voice came from behind her.

"Uh, yes, my friend, I knew it was you—"

The Gidget turned and looked through the shattered porch door at the TV in the living room. She saw Joe on the screen.

"It was you who wrote the book," firmly said Joe. "It was you who ruined Malibu. It was you who told your stepfather about the foam deal. It was you who wanted everything, always did."

A prolonged buzz from a timing device came below the porch. Joe did wire the mansion, The Gidget realized, it's all gonna go.

"Surf's up!" mildly said Joe, adding "Gidget"

"I'm not Gidg...Gidg...Gidg," she gasped.

The explosion welled up from beneath the porch, pulverizing everything into fragments and splinters. A red mist of what was once the lower half of The Gidget vaporized around her. She caught her last ride on a wooden board.

A piercing jet of blackness and flames blasted huge fragments of the Koolner's mansion skyward. The flames from the blast rapidly spread along the dried brush on the hills. Wind carried the flames from roof to roof of the nearby mansions.

"What the fuck?" said Slick, watching the conflagration.

"Oooooh," groaned the wounded old friend, rolling over.

"Crispy!" said Purpus, kneeling over a fading Johnson in the sand. Skip saw the blood. He shrieked, "He's been shot!"

Slick ran over to his wounded friend.

"You're a legend now—run!" said the drunk. Blood bubbled in the corners of his mouth.

"Crispy!" begged Slick.

"I paid you back, you'll see," said the surfer, wincing, his eyes seemed angry, then they softened as he gasped, "Outside."

His eyes became as flat as a dead fish. Crispy was gone. The two surfer stood respectfully silent.

"My wave asshole!" yelled a surfer, colliding with another on a take off.

"Fucking dick!" shouted his foe.

"Eat shit and die!" yelled back the surfer.

Slick and Skip turned to see kooks competitively surfing around the corpses. The surroundings had no effect on the kooks' surfing behavior. They kept burning, snaking, colliding, punching, and swearing at each other. The waves were smaller, they dropped to three feet. The Dead South was dying.

"Check this out," said Purpus, reaching into the wet sand and picking up a one-foot long steatite sculpture of a pointed surfboard. "I guess Joe's back with the Chumash."

Surfer Joe's words returned to Slick: *My board would go into shore without me, and some kook would find it, and a kook would be surfing my board.*

"Shit," said Slick, scowling. "I have to find Joe's board."

"I'll help you."

They ran along the sand's edge toward the pier. Joe's stick was laying fin-up on the rock strewn shore. Not a ding on it.

Some media voices shouted toward Slick.

"That's the guy!"

"The one who rode the wave—"

Slick glanced over. About one hundred feet away, a TV camera crew jogged over to him.

"It's your moment, surf star," said Purpus, gesturing to the media.

Here was Slick's chance to be acknowledged, but he wanted no part of it. Somewhere between the kooks and Malibu Joe got lost in the process, thought Slick, and Joe never forgave himself for it. Slick knew he was heading the same way, but now, he had another break to ride. He had to let Malibu go. It was time to let it all go.

"There's only one King Of Malibu," said Slick, picking up the Simmons board, shaking his head, and smiling. "Shine this, all I want to do is just surf."

The two bros ran off the beach.

Gidget Must Die

Chapter nine

Stoked

Slick spray painted the first few letters on a large rock. A Simmons balsa board leaned against the palm-frond shack's bamboo beams. A crocodile hide dried above the front entrance. There was no door, just a beaded curtain. A rope hammock was slung between two thick poles in the sand. Slick took a bite out of a mango. He scanned the coastline of palm, banyan, and mangrove trees. Monkeys rustled branches. He was the only one on the clean white crescent of sand that opened out into a sparkling aquamarine ocean. A moving corrugation of waves refracted and wrapped parallel to shore. There were two rides to choose from. The mounds hit a reef point, rose in height, split open, and peeled back a ruler-edged topped shoulder for a thousand yards from left to right. And when it simultaneously broke right to left, the wave jacked up six feet on a coral reef, and threw out hollow barrels. The fat-lipped lefts were almost unmakeable. On most days, there weren't lefts. But, today, because of the North swell direction, it was working.

"Slick, mon, you like this one, he beeeg?"

The voice belonged to a dark-skinned pregnant woman. She was a native in her mid-twenties. Hard pearl teeth interspersed with a few brownish ones. Trusting eyes. Luxuriant and long black hair.

She held a huge fish by its tail, a ribbon of blood trickled from a speared opening in its silvery side.

Slick placed his hand upon her belly, and said,"Beautiful."

"Slicky, Slick," said the woman. The brightness in her eyes seemed connected to the energy of her smile.

"With a girl the lonely sea looks good," sang Slick, taking her free arm and slow dancing with her. "Makes your night time warm and out of sight."

She giggled, playfully pushed the fish on him, and laughed. Slick smiled and kissed her. She wandered off.

Slick looked out at Purpus, who was prone paddling a modern longboard Slick shaped him. The board had hard rails in the narrow tail, but the rails softened up in the middle of the board, and hardened into a bevel edge at the tip. It had three fins, a v-bottom, and a slightly pulled-in nose. The stick was nine-feet six inches long and weighed about fifteen pounds.

He saw Purpus spin around and paddle for a sizeable wave. It looked like he was going to risk going left.

Skip Purpus' muscular and dark arms easily stroked deeply through the warm ocean. There were tight cuts and little bulges in his widened shoulders and expansive chest. He had strong upper muscled legs. The chestnut tan made his blue eyes deeper, giving him more depth. His hair was a whitish blonde. His gut was gone. He knew he looked good and he felt damn good about it. He was within all the Malibu pictures he admired: surfing on a longboard, no crowds, and peeling waves. It was everything the Beach Boys sang to him. Skip made it—and he wasn't even wearing a leash. He glided over the undulating pulse line of the ocean's surface toward an outside wave. He quickly spun his board around. The water sucked out in front of him, and rose beneath his board and lifted Skip up to its advancing ridge line. He was offered two choices. The choice on the right was a smooth and easy scenic route. The choice to Skip's left, critical, slightly treacherous but promising, offering a steep takeoff into a curved and throwing wall. As the water travelled up the wave's face, Skip saw reddish coral poke through the shallow water in front of its curling shoulder. It was dumb to go left, ridiculous, suicidal, self-destructive, immature, irresponsible, pointless, insane. But Skip had been working himself up for this ride.

"Reaaaaaaaah," Skip savagely growled, going for it, totally committed.

Purpus cranked the board hard, crouched in a ball, and pulled under the lip as it sliced over him and formed a greenish-blue clamshell. The canopy turned to a whiteness above him. Purpus heard a shoooooosh. He was deep in his first tube, but it looked more like a funnel to him. Skip was at the back of its narrow whirling cone. Eight feet ahead, a three-foot oblong opening dilated. Purpus was getting the vision. Through the tube's opening, he gazed at a curved shoulder of blue that resembled an upper thigh. Behind Skip, the bottom of funnel was caving in, stinging his bare back with its spray. He was so close. Could he make it out, could he?

"Come on, Skip, be somebody," anxiously urged Slick, seeing Purpus' silhouette through the white sheet of water. It looked like the wave was squeezing him out. "Do it."

The tube collapsed, blasting spray from its barrel and spitting out Purpus. Skip skated out onto the blue shoulder, nearly kneeling on the board. He immediately stood, clenched his fists, and triumphantly extended his arms up in the air.

"Score!" shouted Slick.

The two surfers howled simultaneously.

Purpus laid with his back on the deck of his board. He started kicking his legs and flailing his arms around, like a cockroach. Then Skip stood up, and did a reverse kickout, by turning his board to the right, back into the hooking part of the curl, and flying out over it. He held onto his board, plopped on the water, and paddled back out.

"Styling," shouted Slick, laughing. "The kook found some style! You—"

"That's looks like fun," said an uninvited female voice, interrupting the moment. "Could you teach me how to surf?"

Slick whirled around and saw a short, seventeen-year old girl with a pony tail. She wore a thong bathing suit. She had a tight body. Cling peach butt. A flat stomach you could crack an egg on. Small but high-riding breasts. She smiled. Slick gave her the stink eye. He marched to the beach shack, threw the beads of the   curtain back, and disappeared inside. Beads clicked and rattled. Slick emerged with an Uzi.

"Get the fuck out of here!" Slick said, firing the weapon into the sand at the girl's feet.

"I'm leaving, I'm leaving," screeched the girl. She bolted through the thick undergrowth between the palm trees. Her pony tail jiggling.

"Obvee," Slick said, smiling, and firing a round into the air. He stopped, listened. She was gone. Slick put the gun back in the shack. He proudly came out rubbing his hands and confidently declared, "Never again."

Slick started humming a Beach Boys song, grabbed the spray paint can, and wrote out the last few letters on the rock. He stood and read the message.

"Concept," Slick said, picking up the Simmons board, tucking it under his arm, and heading to the waves.

The spray-painted words on the rock were bright orange. Large enough to be read from the water:

Surfer Joe lives

And I do.

If you would like to order a copy of **Gidget Must Die**, please send $16.95 To:

> Santa Cruz'n Press
> PO Box 3523
> Santa Cruz, Ca. 95062

Also, if you'd like to order Fred Reiss' **Insult And Live!**, a 452-page book that teaches you how to identify and slam any loser in and out of the water, just send $17.95 to the above address.

Or, if you'd like to order another great surf book, try **Surfing To Saigon**, by Pat Farley, a raw and true first-person narrative about a California surfer's combat experiences in Vietnam, send $16.25 to the same address. But write the check out to Pat Farley.

Gidget Must Die posters are $7.00.

Santa Cruz'n Longboards Rule t-shirt with picture of the surfer with a gun (Image on table of contents page.) available for $16.95